LONG LIVE
FREEDOM

LONG LIVE FREEDOM

ELIZABETH HUNT

Believer's Dream Publishing

The text of this book is set in 12-point Lucida Sans.
Printed in the United States of America

ISBN: 978-0-9832273-3-5

First edition

First printing, 2014

*For my Parents, my brother,
my extended family and my friends
for always being in my corner.*

CHAPTER 1

Lynton Karter Rider strolled down the road, the high noon sun beating down on his neck as sweat rolled into his eyes. The road kicked up dust with every step, the dirt sticking to Karter's every limb, until he resembled the road so much that birds landed on him to peck for food.

The rambling squeak of wheels on the road sounded behind him and Karter whipped his head up; their steady rhythm was the first city sound he'd heard in nearly a fortnight. The driver of the cart spotted Karter, and he subconsciously ran his hand through his hair which was stiff from dirt and sweat. *Though it probably hasn't changed colors*, Karter thought wryly as the driver approached. His hair was the exact same sandy brown as the dirt road, even when clean.

As the driver rolled past Karter he gave a panicked look and sped up, whipping his donkey into a frenzy in order to pass the roadside vagabond. Karter pursed his lips in annoyance. If the driver had known who he was... But even thinking about his past life made Karter hang his head. He wasn't ever allowed to return to his kingdom of Outeiro. He *was* a vagabond. A homeless teen wandering the road trying in vain to find a city. If only he'd remembered to bring a map. Karter continued walking down the road, wallowing in his misfortune. Why did he have to be the banished twin? Why did he have to be the one to leave Outeiro? Karter kicked a rock in frustration.

Plop! Karter looked up suddenly, recognizing the noise that the rock had made.

"Water," Karter murmured, scanning his surroundings for a hint of the nourishment his frustration had found. A small reflection caught his eye, and Karter stumbled off the road, careless from his thirst.

He knew the tales of water kelpies that dotted the region, but the water and food rations his parents had given him were gone and his throat ached with every step, not to mention his growling stomach. Karter pushed aside some reeds and sighed in satisfaction as the sight of a large pond met his eyes. He dropped his pack down on the bank and staggered into the water, smiling as he felt the cool water seep through his pant-legs, and oblivious to the dangers.

Karter knelt down to drink, washing the dirt off of his arms and legs once he had satisfied his thirst. Once his skin was again the pale color it used to be, he took off his shirt and began to rinse the dirt from it. He was scrubbing and ringing out the shirt, trying in vain to make it resemble the blue it had once been when the ripples began appearing in the middle of the pond. Karter jerked his head up and clambered back up the bank quickly, pulling the sopping shirt back over his head, the cool water against his skin making the hot air suddenly tolerable.

Wagon wheels sounded on the road behind him and Karter quickly fled the pond-side, not even bothering to look up at the wagon as it flew past him, just grateful to be away from the creature in the pond.

Maybe I'm finally near a town, Karter thought as the presence of the cart sunk in. After all, he'd been traveling for two weeks and hadn't seen any carts and suddenly he'd seen two in one day. With a little bit more pep in his step, Karter got back on the road and set off again. A town meant food and shelter and water without monsters.

"You there!" Karter stopped and looked up, surprised to see the wagon that had just passed him sitting in the middle of the road, waiting for him.

"You goin' somewhere?" The driver asked, motioning to Karter's pack.

"Uh, just trying to reach the nearest town sir," Karter responded.

The driver eyed Karter with some suspicion. "The closest town is Conquistado," the driver finally said. "But only a fool would want to go there."

"Do they have food and water for a weary traveler?" Karter asked hopefully as his stomach grumbled audibly.

The driver nodded unhappily. "Aye, they do, but it ain't no hospitable place." The driver spat over the side of the wagon to emphasize his point.

"Are you going there?" Karter asked.

The driver pursed his lips, but nodded. "I have wares to flog."

"Could you please take me with you? I could pay for the transport."

"Boy, you gotta be in some sad straights to be wantin' to go to Conquistado."

Karter just continued to look at the driver hopefully. He was tired of walking and he didn't have the rations to last much longer out here.

"All right, hop in." The driver surrendered, "But don't blame me if what you find ain't to your likin'."

Karter smiled thankfully and jumped into the wagon, slinging his pack into the back and settling down next to the driver.

"What's your name?" The driver asked.

"Rider," Karter answered automatically giving his last name as he was taught. "Karter Rider," he amended, figuring he was far enough from Outeiro that the cart driver wouldn't recognize the name.

"Well, Karter Rider, welcome aboard the wheat express," The driver whipped the donkey forward and Karter settled in for the ride.

"Wake up, son."

Karter jolted awake as the wagon driver shook him.

"What is it?" Karter mumbled, blinking rapidly against the bright setting sun that shone in his eyes.

"We're almost to Conquistado. You gotta be awake to pass through customs."

"Customs?" Karter asked, curious. He'd never had to go through the screening process before. His parent's status had afforded the bypass of such peasantry.

The driver nodded. "Ever since the revolution, the customs o' Conquistado have been a nightmare to go through. If the city didn't provide such good business, I woulda stopped trading here years ago." And without another word, he urged his donkey forward again.

Karter felt his stomach clench as tall gate spires came into view, their stone expanse reaching so high up into the sky they blocked the sun. It was a frighteningly opposing sight, and for the first time, Karter wondered if he should have heeded the cart driver's warning to find a different town.

"State your name and business." A man in armor came up to the cart, his black helmet obscuring his voice so it was difficult to understand him.

"Kaernon. Wheat Seller."

"What about the boy?"

"Karter. Traveler," Karter interrupted before Kaernon could answer.

"Traveling where?" The man asked and Karter could've sworn he narrowed his eyes.

"Here, preferably," Karter answered, though he was almost hoping the soldiers made him turn away. He could practically feel the man in the armor glaring at him. Karter realized it was risky to mouth off to officials, but Karter's family in Outeiro had *owned* the officials. He'd never had reason to fear them before.

"Make trouble and it's the gallows," the armored man said monotonously.

Karter swallowed and nodded. "Yes sir."

The guard backed up and away from the cart as Kaernon urged the donkey forward again. As the cart began to amble down the seemingly empty street, the heavy gates closed with a bang. Karter swallowed audibly. "How long ago was this revolution?" he asked, worriedly.

"Near as I can tell, it's been near ten years since the good city o' Libre was overtaken by Derex Fallon."

"And conditions still haven't improved?" Karter asked. Generally conquered lands relaxed somewhat once their rule was permanently established. At least that's what he'd learned in his studies. The driver stopped the cart so suddenly Karter had to throw his hands forward to prevent himself from flipping out headfirst.

"There are two things you need to know about Conquistado, boy," Kaernon began seriously. "One. It's ruled by a ruthless man. Two. those who ask questions end up dead."

Kaernon urged the donkey forward again leaving Karter sitting there in stunned silence. What kind of land killed newcomers for asking questions? And why on earth had Karter not heeded Kaernon's warning?

Nearly an hour later, when the cart finally pulled into the main square of the town, Karter found some of the people. Used to Outerio's square, Karter was stunned by the difference. The main square in Outeiro was a bustling hub of activity. So much so, carts were banned from entering due to the high congestion of people found along the streets. The main square in Conquistado, however, was barren and nearly devoid of life. Those that did walk along the sidewalks did so with their heads down, dressed in rags so feeble, they threatened to disintegrate with every movement.

"Where is everybody?" Karter asked in a hush, stunned by the sight that befell his eyes.

"There is only one market day a week and that's tomorrow. The people are in their homes. Farming, sewing, darning, cooking... whatever it is they do."

Karter didn't know what to say. "Is market day livelier?" he finally ventured.

"There's more people." Kaernon said simply, and no matter how Karter prodded, that was all he would say on the matter.

The cart drew up beside a run down building with peeling paint reading *Tavern and Inn* just above the door.

"Only place to stay in the entire city," Kaernon grunted as he got down from the driver's seat.

Karter's eyes widened. The place looked condemned. All the buildings did, though the rapidly setting sun probably did not do them any favors.

"You comin', boy?" Kaernon stood in the entrance to the inn, tapping his foot impatiently.

Karter nodded timidly and quickly climbed down from the cart, grabbing his bag as he went and clutching it like a lifeline.

The inside of the tavern wasn't much better than the outside. Tables sat empty and derelict while a lone man polished glasses behind a wide counter.

"Ahh, Kaernon," the barman said when he looked over his shoulder. "The usual room is open. I left the key by that table over there. Knew you'd be by sooner or later."

Kaernon walked over to the table and picked up a rusted key on a small leather band.

"I'll also need a room for this young lad here; picked him up on the road. He needs a place to stay until he can find a ride to the next town."

The barman whipped around in surprise.

"Well, will you look at that. 'Bout time a new soul came into this godforsaken land." The barman hustled around to the counter and went over to a small desk in the corner that Karter hadn't noticed before. After digging around for a while, the man pulled out a key that was nearly black with rust, the leather band full of holes and crumbling into pieces as he held it.

"Here you go; I kept this just in case someone ever came around that wasn't a regular. Glad I did."

Karter took the disintegrating object carefully, doing his best not to wrinkle his nose as its pungent moldy smell met his nostrils.

"I have the crew clean the room still, so don't you worry about that. And you probably can't tell anymore, but it's the key to room 13. All the way at the top of the inn."

Karter nodded, hoping this place had no bedbugs. He looked around for Kaernon to thank him, but the man had disappeared. So much for that.

"Where are the stairs?" Karter asked the retreating barman's back.

"Oh, sorry, they're right through that door over there," the barman said, looking slightly flustered.

Karter nodded his thanks and went to push open the door. It led to a small hallway with two doors and a rickety stair case spiraling up into the ceiling. Karter put his hand against the stair railing and pushed, relieved when it didn't give way. Gingerly, he began climbing the stairs, wincing every time they groaned. The walls were thin, and every time the wind whipped, a howling could be heard from some crack as the wind found its way into the house. Karter grit his teeth as a particularly large gust caused the house and staircase to sway.

At least it's shelter, Karter reminded himself as he finally reached the top of the staircase and faced the rotting door to his room. He put the decrepit key in the lock and turned it very carefully, hoping dearly that it wouldn't break. To his relief, the key opened the lock with ease, and the door swung open, revealing a clean cot and a small dresser in a room no larger than the two furniture items.

Karter squeezed into the room and sat down on the cot, biting his lip to keep the tears from spilling. The last time he'd had a bed to sleep in had been the night before he turned seventeen and it had been ten times more ornate than this hellhole. He briefly wondered if his family missed him but quickly pushed the thought from his mind.

"It doesn't matter," he muttered.

Still fighting to keep the memories of his past from filling his mind, Karter laid his head down on the flat pillow and drifted off to sleep.

Karter awoke to the sound of drums coming through the window and bright sunlight streaming down onto his bed. The light lit up the dust motes, and for a while Karter lay there, watching them create patterns above his head. Then a cloud passed in front of the sun, cloaking Karter's room in darkness once again. Karter sighed heavily and got out of bed, struggling to get over to the window in the narrow room. Below him, the main square had indeed been transformed. In the clouded daylight, the buildings no longer looked shabby and derelict, but well-built and lived in. The grey streets were lit with colored lanterns and though they weren't dressed much better, Kaernon had been right. There *were* more people. So many people that Karter had trouble distinguishing one person from the next while they were grouped so closely together.

Then Karter noticed the soldiers. All around the market, guarding every entrance to the main square, were soldiers dressed in the same black armor as the ones at the gate the previous day.

What a strange town, Karter thought. Then he shrugged and grabbed his pack. Surely in the market he could find a way to move on to a decent town.

Down in the street, the market was pure chaos. Everywhere Karter looked stalls were set up with wares of all kinds, each owner trying to out shout his neighbor. Karter recognized Kaernon selling bread in a slightly more secluded area of the market where people could be distinguished from the mob.

"Excuse me." Two girls pushed past Karter roughly as they tried to make it through the crowd. Karter raised his eyebrows in surprise as he took in their retreating backs. They were both dressed in long cloaks and their hair looked like it'd been smeared with mud. As Karter watched, a soldier glanced toward the girls and they both ducked quickly.

Strange, Karter thought, furrowing his eyebrows. His curiosity overcoming him, he tried to follow the two strangers. Several minutes later, however, Karter had to admit he had lost them. With a frustrated sigh, he turned to the nearest stall and got in line, hoping the owner would be able to give him directions, or at least tell him where he could get a map. He needed to get out of here.

"Yes sir, may I help you?" asked a middle-aged man who looked rather decrepit.

"Um, yes, I was hoping you could tell me where I could find a ride to the next town."

The stall owner laughed dryly. "Boy, the only way out of here is death." Shooing Karter aside, the stall owner began to help the next customer.

Karter huffed—he just needed a map.

Maybe Kaernon knows someone. Karter thought, moving back through the wall to wall crowd in an effort to find the cart driver.

"Excuse me, pardon me, let me through please," Karter said repeatedly as he struggled to shove his way through the crowd. He finally pushed through the last few people and found himself in a clear spot right next to a pair of stocks, nowhere near the corner where Kaernon had been.

Karter looked up, his grumbling silenced in shock as he suddenly found himself face to face with a young boy of about twelve, his arms and head locked into the wooden prison. The boy looked at Karter with pleading eyes and Karter grimaced in sympathy. He wondered what crime the boy had committed to deserve such brutal treatment. He must've been quite the criminal to deserve such a fate. *A pity at such a young age.*

Karter furrowed his eyebrows as he noticed the boy's shirt was covered in muddy leaves, and his pants looked like blue burlap.

What a strange outfit, Karter thought as he began to back away from the boy and attempt to meld back into the crowd. That's when Karter noticed the other stock. In it was one of the strange girls he had seen earlier that he'd been unable to follow. Karter looked closer and then stared unceremoniously. The girl was only pretending to be in the stocks! The wooden prison wasn't locked. His heart racing, Karter wondered what was going on with this town. The boy seemed to finally notice that there was someone in the stock next to him and his eyes widened in recognition.

"Sam, get me out of here," he hissed.

The girl shot the boy a warning look, jerking her head pointedly toward Karter.

Karter felt his blood boil. He may not have known much about this town, but in *his* city, nobody was put in the stocks without an extraordinarily good reason. Releasing someone in the stocks was a worse crime than murder because odds were, the person you released *had* committed murder.

"Guards!" Karter yelled, whatever was up, it was right to stop it. The girl in the stocks widened her eyes and started shaking her head "no".

"Guards!" Karter yelled again, turning around to see them. "Whoa!" Karter yelped as he turned around right into the other strange girl who promptly slapped him across the face.

"Get out of there, Sam, the guards are coming."

"We have time; it'll take them forever to get through that mob," Sam replied, detangling herself from the stock.

"I don't want to take that chance, secrecy is gone," the second girl bit back using a short sword to chop the lock off the boy's stock. "Run," she told him. The boy nodded and took off.

"What about this fool?" Sam asked, jerking her head toward Karter.

The second girl bit her lip. Karter just stood there like a fool, hoping she wouldn't slap him again. These girls were not your average villagers, that much was obvious. In the turmoil, their cloaks had fallen off of them a bit, revealing the exact same clothes the boy had been wearing. What had he gotten himself into?

"We'll take him with us," the second girl finally said.

"Whoa, what?" Karter asked, but the girls ignored him.

"But—" Sam started to protest, but the second girl cut her off.

"He's a stranger, they'll lock him up if they realize he let us get away."

"I'm sorry, did you say, "lock up?"" Karter tried to clarify, but the girls were still talking as if he couldn't hear them.

"That still doesn't mean we should help him," Sam muttered, but she took one of Karter's hands ignoring his protests. The second girl took his other hand, and together they began to drag him out of the market place toward the forest.

"Now wait just a minute," Karter said, breathing in relief when they finally seemed to hear him. "Now, I don't particularly want to come with you," he began. "I really just want a map."

The girls exchanged annoyed glares. And Karter had just enough time to yank his hands free before Sam hit him on the head and everything went black.

CHAPTER 2

Alick Karenza Daveney snuck through the woods, her hands around the ankles of the stranger from the market. Behind her, Sam had the boy's shoulders, not being particularly careful whether he hit the ground or not. In the distance, the guards were yelling, trying to follow the two slippery thieves. But Alick didn't worry. The guards never followed them into the forest. Why should today be any different?

"When do you think he'll wake up?" Alick asked her friend as they reached the first outpost of their camp. They set the boy down on the ground to rest their muscles. He was much heavier than he looked.

Sam shrugged and rolled her eyes. "I didn't hit him that hard. He should be awake already."

Alick sighed and tried not to roll her eyes back. "What should we do with him?" she asked under her breath. When she'd suggested they bring him along, Alick hadn't really thought much beyond keeping him safe. He was clearly an outsider, and Fallon did not take well to outsiders. She was surprised he even made it into the kingdom alive.

"Hey, you're the one that wanted to bring him with us. You gotta decide what to do with him."

"Need help?" Robin asked as he jumped out of a nearby tree.

"Yeah, help us carry this lump," Sam said gesturing to the stranger on the ground.

"He the one that almost upset the mission?"

"So Layne made it back to camp?" Alick asked, referring to the boy they'd rescued from the stocks.

"Yup, you'd think since we rescued him from the gallows the first time he'd take more care not to keep getting caught." Robin muttered, helping them pick up the stranger again. Alick just smiled, she understood the frantic energy that often possessed the younger kids.

"We'll just assign him duties closer to the forest in the future," Sam answered, resignedly.

"He's really too young to be scouting in the village anyway."

"You're telling me! You guys won't even let *me* go out there. And I'm Peter's second in command."

Alick let out a small laugh and Robin stuck his tongue out at her. It was true Robin was technically fourth in command, but he was only fourteen. Too young to have any true responsibilities running the Pantasmas. It was good for Peter to have a protégée, though; it reminded him that the world didn't revolve around the great and glorious Peter. There were others who could get hurt if he was pig-headed.

"We're back!" Alick called as they finally came into the main clearing.

She was met by cheers and calls as her followers welcomed her home. Alick smiled again. It felt good to be back where she belonged. Since she'd escaped to the forest as a child, the city had felt foreign and hostile. Alick dropped the stranger's leg, and Sam and Robin followed suit.

"Who's this?" Peter, asked as he came up to them jerking his head toward the stranger.

Alick shrugged. "No idea," she sighed. "He's new to town and got in the way of our mission."

Peter nodded and ordered Robin back to his post.

"What's the situation look like?" Alick asked Peter. She moved away with him where they wouldn't be overhead, conscious of Sam standing guard over the stranger to keep the curious Pantasmas at bay.

"The men building the wall around the city are drawing closer with each day. Based on their trajectory, we think they're going to cut through the forest about five miles south of here. When they arrive, we'll have to be very careful and maybe even move camp."

Alick sighed, but nodded. "All right. Any other situations?"

Peter looked down and shifted his weight nervously.

"What is it, Peter?" Alick asked impatiently.

"Heritor Day is coming," Peter finally said in a low voice. He shuffled his feet uncomfortably as if waiting for Alick to explode.

Alick felt as if her heart had dropped to her feet. "You're kidding," she whispered back.

Peter shook his head. "No, Alick, I'm not."

"Alick, come quick, he's waking." Sam called from her place by the stranger.

"We'll discuss this later, Peter," Alick muttered. She jogged back to Sam and dropped to her knees beside the stranger just as he opened his eyes.

"Who are you?" Alick asked aggressively when the stranger had fully come to his senses.

The stranger looked warily around him as if trying to determine whether or not he could run. Sam, in response, took out her dagger and casually began cleaning her boots with it.

Alick suppressed a laugh when the stranger's face paled. He clearly was not used to such rough country.

"What is your name?" Alick tried again in a kinder tone.

"Karter," the stranger said, sitting up. "My name's Karter." His eyes shifted around the camp, processing his situation.

"Where are you from, Karter?" Alick asked.

"It doesn't matter," Karter muttered, looking around again. "Where am I?"

Poor boy looked so confused, Alick felt her heart thump sympathetically.

"The Pantasma camp. Welcome," Rydly, Alick's other best friend, said, coming up behind them.

"This is *our* interrogation, Riddle," Sam snapped.

"I just came to welcome Alick home and to offer our prisoner some *cordial* company," Rydly bit back. The two of them began bickering as Alick sighed and rolled her eyes. Her friends could never get along.

She turned back to Karter and held out her hand to help him up.

"I'm Alick," she said to Karter as they stood up. "You can stay here with us. Rydly will show you the ropes." Alick reached behind her and forcibly yanked Rydly around, ending the argument.

"Where is here?" Karter whispered to Rydly as he took his wrist and led him off to the fire, explaining the history of the camp as he went and leaving Alick, Sam, and Peter off to the side by themselves.

"Peter, how soon is Heritor Day?" Alick asked, ignoring Sam when she gasped.

"Tomorrow."

"That soon?" Sam asked.

Peter nodded. "And we're *all* expected to be in the town square watching. Just in case." Peter emphasized the *all* and looked pointedly at Alick.

Alick put her head in her hands. Heritor Day was supposed to be a day of celebration, a day when a new ruler was selected at random. But none of the Pantasmas were welcome in the village, and Derex Fallon was unlikely to let anybody else be King, ever.

"We'll have to carry weapons in our clothes. Dress nicely to blend in better. Nobody really knows who's who in our band of thieves. They mostly just recognize us by our clothing." Alick began muttering plans to herself. It was times like this when she absolutely hated being in charge. It was a crushing burden to be responsible for so many in such dangerous times.

"What about Ashton, Ashley, and I?" Sam asked. "We were born in the forest; we won't be on the roster."

"You probably will be, Sam. You have your own "wanted" sign," Peter said wryly.

Sam punched his arm.

"We can't leave Ashton and Ashley alone in the forest; they're only 8. We'll have to take them with us," Alick responded absentmindedly as her thoughts whirred about the safest way to follow tradition and remain unscathed.

Sam looked over Alick's shoulder and smiled. "I forgot about somebody."

"Who?" Alick asked, distractedly staring at the maps Peter had laid out and thinking about anything else they could do to blend into the city better.

"Piper," Sam said, wiggling her eyebrows mischievously.

Alick's eyes widened and she turned around just in time to catch the five-year old hurling toward her.

"Hey Piper," she said, laughter in her eyes as she spun the girl around, the present crisis pushed to the back of her mind. "How are you?"

"Good," the little girl replied, smiling wide. "I found a mushroom *this* big." She held her arms out to show Alick the size of her mushroom.

"Really?" Alick asked while behind her Sam laughed quietly. "Was it poisonous?" Alick asked Piper in a stage whisper.

"No, silly," Piper crowed. "There are no poisonous mushrooms around here."

"But surely one *that* big would just *have* to be bad," Alick pointed out playfully.

"No," Piper said again.

"If you say so," Alick sang.

Piper stuck her tongue out and ran off, hurdling over a log.

Alick watched her go with a pang of sadness. Piper had been born in the forest, too, and had never been outside of it. Heritor Day was going to be a nightmare.

"Sometimes I wish Fallon could just father a child and rid us of this mess."

"Even Fallon can't live forever. We're better off without any devil spawn, even if it does mean we have to follow tradition."

CHAPTER 3

"So, where are you from?" Rydly asked as he led Karter away from Sam and Alick.

"It doesn't matter," Karter said quickly, tripping over a root and nearly doing a face plant into a leaf pile.

Rydly looked over at him and raised his eyebrows. "It matters a little. You're obviously not from around here."

"Is it that obvious?" Karter asked, slightly sullen, as he sat down on a moss covered log. He couldn't believe it was only yesterday that he'd been walking along the dusty road.

Rydly sat down next to him and smiled. "Well, first off, you got in the way of Alick and Sam's mission. Nobody does that. Except the soldiers, of course. Second, you're about our age.

If you were from here, you'd be dead, already a Pantasma, or working on Fallon's 'wall'."

Karter blinked heavily. All Rydly had done whilst explaining was fill Karter's head with more questions.

"Who's Fallon and what are the Pantasmas?" Karter asked first, figuring it was most important to know whom he was with.

"Derex Fallon, dictator of Conquistado. 'Bout ten years ago he conquered Libre, killed the king, and took over. He's made our lives miserable ever since. The Pantasmas are us," Rydly gestured to the group of boys and girls that bustled about the camp, "we're rebels, so to speak. We live here in the forest separate from Fallon's rule."

Karter nodded vaguely, not really paying attention anymore. He remembered Kaernon telling him about the revolution. "And his 'wall'?" Karter put air quotes around wall just like Rydly had.

Rydly sighed and got up, grabbing a bushel of firewood and motioning for Karter to do the same. "His wall is a twenty foot high stone structure being built around the city by every able-bodied man Fallon can find. They're let off in shifts so about twenty men are present in the village at all times. But fewer and fewer are coming back. The wall is consuming their lives. Endless labor, rough conditions..." Rydly shook his head. "Fallon claims the wall is to protect us from enemies. But everybody knows that when it's completed, not only will it not let anybody *in* the city, the wall won't allow anybody *out* either." Rydly threw his firewood down next to the fire and began to feed the flames.

Karter sat down next to him and mulled over what Rydly had just told him. He was seriously considering running for it, but if what Rydly said was true, then he'd likely be caught by Fallon's soldiers, and the last thing he wanted was to be arrested.

A child's high voice carried over the crackling of the flames. Karter looked around and spotted a small girl talking to Alick about a mushroom she had found. Karter blinked heavily and then looked again. The small girl was still there. "How old is she?" Karter asked, turning to Rydly.

Rydly looked up, confused. "Who?" he asked.

"The small girl over there by Alick."

Rydly craned his neck to where Karter was pointing and smiled. "That's Piper, she's five."

"Five," Karter repeated, stunned.

"Yeah, why?"

"What is this place, Rydly? You said it's a rebel group. But..." Karter focused on the people and things in the camp properly for the first time. Several tents were arranged in a semi circle around the fire whilst behind them a creek gurgled. Around the woods, mostly on the outset of the camp, children played while teens watched them, fixed up clothing, or practiced sword play and archery. Lookouts were spaced evenly between the trees and up in the foliage perhaps ten feet apart. At first glance, the camp was every bit like the military outposts Karter had visited with his father and brother, but there couldn't have been a single person over the age of twenty-five. "Everyone is so young," Karter finished. It was astonishing. Karter would bet half the lookouts weren't yet sixteen.

"In the beginning," he started as he fed the flames, "It was just Alick, Sam, and I. We roamed the forest free from Fallon's rule. We were just kids, lawless orphans making it on our own. Then we began to find others in the woods. Peter," Rydly pointed to the built guy who had been talking to Alick and Sam earlier, "and Tara and Kara," he pointed to two girls, a tall one with jet black hair and another slightly smaller one with fairer skin and chestnut hair.

"They were the first three to join us. Through the years we've amassed about a hundred followers, other orphans, village kids whose families were ripped asunder. The youngest is Sally. She's about three. Peter's the oldest. He's about twenty." Rydly was quiet for a bit. "We rescue them, Karter. We save them from Fallon and we keep them here. Safe from harm. We're no rebel group, though we call it that. We don't really rebel against anything. The riskiest thing we do is free Fallon's prisoners and steal supplies to keep us alive. Most of the time, he lets us. We are not a threat to him... At least we weren't."

"What do you mean?"

"As we get older, Fallon's been looking for us more. If our group gets old enough, we could be a serious threat to his reign. Fallon knows this. And he's beginning to do some things about it. It's becoming a very dangerous thing to be a Pantasma."

Karter swallowed audibly. He found himself wondering once again what he had gotten himself into and whether he could still escape.

"Rydly, who exactly is Fallon, besides a dictator-king?"

"None of us really know. Not in this camp anyway. We were too young when he took over.

The first I heard of him was when he came to this kingdom to court the Queen's younger sister. About a month before the wedding, he led an uprising, and his followers killed just about everyone in the castle that wasn't loyal to him. He's been in charge ever since."

"You, new guy," the second girl came over and motioned to Karter.

"He has a name, Samantha," Rydly called back grumpily from his place near the fire with an automatic air.

"I didn't ask you, Riddle, and *don't* call me Samantha," the girl said as she whacked Rydly on the back of his head.

She turned to Karter and handed him a sword. Karter looked down at the dull hilt with confusion.

"What's the matter? Never seen a sword before? Come on." Sam turned and walked away.

Karter blinked and looked at Rydly.

"You should follow her," he said resignedly.

Karter got up and followed Sam over to a clear area slightly beyond the camp. By the looks of the leaves on the ground, it was a common place to go.

Sam's hair was still smeared with mud and her clothes were torn and dirty, but there was something powerful about her and the way she commanded everyone. Karter looked back down at the sword in his hand and wondered what he was supposed to do with it since he could clearly never win a duel against this girl.

Without warning, Sam pulled a sword from the sheath at her hip and attacked, forcing Karter to do his best to defend himself. He knew it was only a matter of time till she overcame him; Karter had often watched his brother, Balthazar, during his sword practice, but this was the first time Karter had been handed a sword himself and been expected to fight.

All of his ideas about sword fighting being easily learned simply by watching were quickly extinguished. Within seconds, Sam knocked his sword away and pinned him to the ground, a stick poking painfully up into his back.

"Wow," Sam said, getting up. She sounded slightly amazed. "You're even weaker than Rydly." She walked back into camp and shouted, "Riddle, he's with you." Then she ducked into a tent.

Karter got up slowly, nursing the bruises he'd acquired in the brief skirmish. He was so confused. He scanned the camp for Alick, but she seemed to have disappeared.

Rydly came over and looked at him with some amusement.

"I have no idea what's going on," Karter said honestly.

Rydly laughed. "Come on, it's almost dinner time. I'll try to explain."

Together they walked back into the center of camp, passing tents and Pantasmas scurrying to clean up, until they came to a large pot surrounded by logs. Rydly sat down upon the closest one, and Karter hesitantly sat next to him. It was beginning to grow dark, and the setting sun shone brilliantly through the trees, lighting the leaves in a surreal orange that contrasted sharply with their usual green.

"What do you want to know?" Rydly asked.

"What just happened?" Karter replied, still dazed—maybe he'd hit his head when Sam pinned him.

Rydly smiled wryly. "In the Pantasmas, everybody over the age of eight has a job. Sam was evaluating you for yours."

"Sam's the leader?" Karter asked. It seemed somewhat likely. She seemed to be forceful enough.

Rydly snorted. "Nah, she's second in command."

Karter looked at Rydly questioningly.

"Sam is definitely the more violent of the two, but Alick is in charge. She was the first, so she's the leader of the Pantasmas. There's a fair amount of delegation, but any large issue gets presented to her." Karter let that sink in. The nice girl was the leader, and the touchy girl was second in command.

"So... what's my job?" Karter asked, since that would be important.

"Well, since you're completely inept at swordplay... no offense."

Karter shrugged; it was a little offensive, but it was also the sad truth. As the weaker twin, no one had ever bothered to teach him much of anything since he wouldn't ever be good for anything.

"Sam has assigned you to work with me."

"And what do you do?"

"I am virtually the maid," Rydly grumbled. "Since the older girls are either fighting or watching the children, I get to do all of the busywork," Rydly said only somewhat bitterly.

"Why does she call you Riddle?" Karter blurted out. "Do you know any?" It was a rude question, but Karter was curious.

Rydly looked up, taken aback. "We've never gotten along. It's just one of the names she calls me. And no, I suck at riddles."

"But you're both Alick's friends."

"And that means we have to be friends too?" Rydly asked, his eyebrows raised.

Karter frowned. He'd never really thought about it like that before. He'd never had a friend, only siblings. Fortunately, he was spared from answering Rydly as the dinner bell rang out loudly, echoing around the camp. Karter wondered how the town didn't hear it, then almost fell backward from fright as a hundred or so kids came running toward the large cauldron in front of Rydly in a large mob, all fighting to be the first to get food.

Rydly looked over at him, slightly amused. "They won't hurt you," he mouthed over the din.

Karter narrowed his eyes and then blushed from embarrassment. He'd never realized how unprepared for the real world his upbringing had made him, and now here he was, in the middle of a rebel camp, a prince among thieves. Karter sighed nervously and began helping Rydly serve the camp. It was going to take a while to get used to this new life. It was frightening to consider living in the woods, but Karter felt he could do some good here and he'd never been much good for anything before.

CHAPTER 4

The moon was almost peeking over the trees when Alick finally sat down beside the fire to eat. Around her, some of her Pantasmas still ate, savoring their meal. The rest had dispersed for their nightly activities. The vague shouts of the younger ones playing tag in the woods echoed through the night.

"Here, I saved you some bread." Rydly and Karter appeared out of the smoke, Rydly carrying a small slice of the tough substance that passed as bread and Karter carrying a bowl of hot soup. Alick took the bread gratefully; despite its coarse nature, it was still enjoyable. Besides, she hadn't had real bread in almost a decade; she couldn't even really remember what it looked like, let alone what it tasted like.

"Where's Sam?" Rydly asked, sitting down next to her. He looked tired.

"No idea, I think she's on border patrol tonight."

"Shouldn't you know where your friends go?" Karter asked her, obviously confused. Alick tilted her head to one side; she wondered for the thousandth time which kingdom he came from and why he'd come here of all places. Surely there were thousands of other cities he'd rather be in.

"We've known each other for almost our entire lives. We're more like sisters than friends. Did you ever have siblings?" Alick watched Karter's face carefully as the question registered. First he turned paler, then his face went red. Alick narrowed her eyes.

"Six," he muttered, turning so his eyes wouldn't meet hers.

Alick looked at Rydly questioningly, but he just shrugged. For the first time, she wondered if it was safe to have brought Karter into the Pantasma camp.

Alick shrugged off the thought and went back to her stew. She was generally a good judge of character, and though Karter was strange, she didn't think he was dangerous. But he was definitely hiding *something*. Alick took a bite of her stew and hummed contentedly. Rydly had done a fantastic job tonight. The stew had bits of meat and plenty of vegetables, some from the little gardens they cultivated and others scrounged from the woods. She remembered many a stomachache from her childhood before they figured out which mushrooms were good to eat. It was pure luck she'd never eaten anything deadly.

As she ate, Alick watched Karter out of the corner of her eye, thinking. Sam said he had utterly failed the sword test, but he was clearly no stranger to sword craft. Now, sitting in the dark, there was definite regal-like nature to the way he held himself. She had first noticed it in the market. It was one of the three reasons she'd known on the spot he was foreign, the other two being that Alick didn't recognize him—she knew everybody—and his spirit wasn't broken. Even among the Pantasmas it was rare to find someone unaffected by Fallon's rule. But Karter carried a different kind of weight upon his shoulders, and she longed to discover what it was.

Movement made Alick look up. Rydly had gotten up and left to do something, leaving Karter looking indecisive. Again, Alick felt her heart beat sympathetically the same way it would if she came across a baby bird fallen from its nest.

"Has Rydly introduced you?" Alick asked.

Karter jumped, obviously surprised at being addressed. Alick smiled.

"Um, to who?" Karter asked nervously.

"The Pantasmas," Alick replied simply, taking another bite of stew.

Karter shook his head. "I just know you, Sam, Rydly, Piper, Peter, Tara, Kara, and Sally."

Alick smiled again. Karter was so earnest, it was strange. She wasn't used to such treatment.

"All right, then," she started kindly, "Well, Rydly probably told you that I'm the leader of the Pantasmas, right?"

Karter nodded nervously. He seemed wary of power. Definitely strange; most in Conquistado would seize it without question.

"Well, Sam's second in command. Peter, he's our general, is third in command. Robin," Alick pointed out the young boy, "is Peter's protégée—so technically fourth in command—"

"Where does Rydly fit in? If he's been here as long as you and Sam, shouldn't he be important?" Karter interrupted.

Alick shrugged. "Really, all we have are the warriors, mostly boys, and then the rest of them."

"And Rydly's one of the 'rest of them'?"

Alick nodded with a small laugh. "Rydly's many things—he'd probably be a respectable leader—but against Fallon, all leaders need to fight and Rydly's no warrior."

"Is that because he's weak?" Karter asked, tentatively Alick shot her head up, surprised.

"What makes you say he's weak?" she asked, her mind racing.

"Sam."

"Oh," Alick exclaimed, the comment suddenly making sense. "Sam only appreciates physical strength. The strength it takes to kill. A warrior's strength." Alick knew she sounded bitter, but she didn't care. She didn't like that she and her friends were forced to sometimes take a life in order to spare their own. It was a twisted world.

"Do you have that strength?" Karter didn't sound judgemental or concerned. He sounded... Alick thought about his voice. He almost sounded pensive. He *wanted* her to say no. Alick couldn't blame him. It was an alarming topic.

Alick tilted her head and looked into Karter's eyes, trying to decide how to answer. All she really accomplished, though, was notice his eyes were hazel.

"Hey, Alick!" Peter called, startling Alick out of her reverie.

"Yes?" she asked, looking up and trying to hide how annoyed she felt at the interruption. She was dreadfully curious about Karter's past and was just about to ask him about it.

"Where are the chests?" he asked. Alick bit her lip.

"Um, I think they're in the back of Tent 6."

Peter nodded and moved off.

"Chests?" Karter asked.

Alick sighed. Sometimes she hated being in charge. It was difficult to ever have a private conversation all the way through. "They're giant wooden crates of clothing we've gotten from the village. Anytime an outfit makes its way into camp that isn't dark blue burlap pants and camouflaged shirts, it goes into the crates."

"Why does Peter want them?"

"Tomorrow, we're going to town."

"Again?" Karter asked, clearly alarmed. "But isn't it dangerous?"

Alick sighed. "We really don't have much of a choice this time, though, yes, it is quite dangerous."

"Then why are we going?"

"Law."

"I thought you lived outside Fallon's rule?"

"There are some laws that cannot be ignored. This particular law predates Fallon by thousands of years. No one has ever ignored it and no one ever will. Not even Fallon. There are powers in this world even he fears." Alick stood up and handed her bowl to the nearest Pantasma. It was time she went to bed.

"Alick, wake up. Wake up, Alick!"

Alick blinked groggily up into the eyes of Sam, who was insistently shaking her shoulder.

"Finally, I thought I was going to have to spray you with water or something," Sam said just as Alick managed to focus.

"What time is it?" Alick asked, shoving her face back into the pillow. She was trying to remember the dream she'd been having. It had been quite peaceful—a nice change from the usual nightmares.

"Midmorning. We have to start getting everyone ready," Sam said, pulling back the tent flaps. The morning sun streamed into the tent and right into Alick's eyes.

Alick groaned. Why did today have to be Heritor Day?

"You know, you're going to have to get up eventually."

Alick ignored Sam, letting the sun lie across her face, warming her. The cot was so nice and comfortable.

Suddenly a loud splash sounded outside.

Alick sat bolt upright, instantly awake. "What was that?" she asked, scrambling up and pulling on her Pantasma outfit.

Sam ducked her head out of the tent. "I think Peter just fell into the river," her friend said, sounding amused and not nearly concerned as she should have been. People did not just *fall* into rivers.

Alick shook her head. Why couldn't she just have one moment's peace? She rolled up her sleeping blankets to keep the bugs out and stepped out into the sunshine, shielding her eyes until they adjusted to the bright sun.

Around her, chaos was ensuing. The normal morning activities were being carried out by the older children while Peter tried to convince the younger children that they needed to wash up.

It was not going well for him. Everywhere Alick looked, screaming children ran around, ducking laundry buckets and water pails and the warriors attempting to catch the children for their baths.

"Hmm," Sam said from behind Alick. "Maybe I shouldn't have left them alone with him."

Alick turned around and raised her eyebrows, trying not to laugh, no longer as alarmed as she had been a minute ago. No one was hurt. No one was in danger.

"What?" Sam asked, shrugging. "It didn't seem like that bad of an idea—" Sam was cut off as she had to stumble back quickly to avoid being trampled by a particularly burly warrior chasing Piper. "—at the time," Sam finished, growling slightly.

Alick shook her head in amusement. Sometimes she was surprised the Pantasmas could even function. Peter was certainly no good with the children, and many of the warriors operated purely on keeping the camp safe from outsiders, not laying a hand toward making sure it was safe on the inside.

She walked to the center of the camp and stood up on the cauldron that had been upended to dry. From her higher vantage point, the chaos was even more pronounced. With a sigh, Alick put her fingers into her mouth and whistled as loud as she could.

A gunshot could not have produced a better reaction.

As Alick's whistle reverberated around the camp, all activity came to a stop.

Alick nodded appreciatively. It had taken her a long time to perfect that little trick.

"Excellent," she said. Then she cleared her throat and projected her voice. "Today is Heritor Day. I need everyone to scrub themselves clean and then come to the center clearing for proper clothing. Once you have done that, continue with your chores if you have them and sit around the fire circle if you do not. *Do not* get dirty again. It's a nice occasion and the goal is to blend in. Sticking out is dangerous, and we're not going to lose anyone today. Any questions?"

Alick waited, but nobody raised their hand. "Go on, then." Alick shooed away her audience, then climbed down from the cauldron. That had been easier than she thought. Normally they put up a greater fuss about cleaning themselves. The chaos had proven that. Perhaps she'd frightened them with talk of losing people. Or they were just more nervous than she was, and the chaos had been an excess of nerves expressing themselves. With a shrug, Alick began assisting the progress.

With any luck, they'd make it through this unscathed. Unfortunately, luck was a rare thing to come by.

CHAPTER 5

arter watched in awe as Alick managed to take complete control of what been complete chaos. The rowdy children were suddenly perfectly obedient as the weary-looking older girls helped the littlest ones clean themselves up whilst the other children took turns jumping into the river and scrubbing the dirt off of their hands and feet. It was a miracle. Karter lowered the bucket of water he was holding and caught Rydly's eye over the sea of people.

Rydly smirked and walked over. "Impressive, right?"

"I'll say," Karter muttered. He had never seen order so neatly assembled except for perhaps in the militia. "Um...what's Heritor Day?"

he asked as he stuck his arms into the bucket of water he had just set down and began to scrub.

"Heritor Day is an ancient solution to the lack of an heir."

"How could there not be anyone in line for the throne?" Karter asked.

"Fallon doesn't have any children," Rydly said with a shrug.

"What about close relatives, a niece, a nephew, cousin? There's always *someone*." Karter was completely flabbergasted. In his kingdom, the succession went like fifty deep. There would never be any situation where that wasn't true.

"Fallon killed the King and his wife when he took over ten years ago. The old King didn't have any siblings, and his parents were long dead. The Queen had one sister, Fallon's wife—"

"So Fallon does actually have a legitimate claim to the throne? He did marry the Queen's sister after all?" Karter interrupted.

Rydly nodded. "Yeah, after the take-over, to help maintain his rule. Which, of course, makes dispatching him all the more difficult."

"Okay. So... Fallon doesn't have any siblings that could take the throne? There aren't any fifth cousins of the king or something?"

"Nope. No siblings, and no issue. And anyone with a remote claim to the throne through the old king's bloodline left decades ago with no way to find them, or has been since executed by Fallon."

"And the old king didn't have any children?"

Rydly shifted around awkwardly, quite obviously trying to avoid the question. Karter narrowed his eyes. Why was Rydly acting so suspicious?

"Let's just say if King Alexander's child had escaped Fallon...there would still be no way Fallon would ever let that kid be a ruler," Rydly finally said in a low undertone. With a facial expression that clearly said "drop it."

Karter furrowed his eyebrows in confusion. "Wait, Fallon killed the old king's only kid?"

"Riddle! Carrot!" Sam yelled from across the clearing.

Rydly pursed his lips. "Oh look, the beast gave you a nickname."

"I never did like carrots," Karter said without meaning to, causing Rydly to snort.

"The two of you need to hurry up. Alick and I need your help handing out clothes."

Karter looked at Rydly and raised his eyebrows.

"Fine, but you know we're not your servants," Rydly complained to Sam, getting up.

Karter rolled his eyes and followed Rydly. He didn't understand why Rydly let Sam push him around so much. She was a girl. Yes, she happened to be an extremely abrasive and violent girl, and his superior... okay maybe he did understand. But Rydly could at least do something other than glare at her. In Karter's mind, Rydly and Sam should be equal since they were equally close to Alick.

"Thanks for coming to help, guys," Alick greeted them as they reached her.

Karter smiled; at least someone appreciated him and Rydly.

"No problem, Alick. How can we assist?" Karter asked, ignoring Rydly's pointed look.

"Can you look through these trunks and try to sort the clothes? It's slow going with just one," she said with a sigh.

"Into what categories?" Rydly replied.

"Um, young girls, young boys, and older girls, and older boys," Alick said, furrowing her eyebrows and pointing at the paltry piles she'd already started.

Karter shrugged and got to work, letting his thoughts swirl like snowflakes, dizzying and jumbled, their shape uncertain. Did Fallon really kill his nephew/niece as well as his/her parents, and *everyone* of that bloodline he could find?

Why did his wife still love him even if she knew Fallon had killed her sister? Was she behind the massacre? What kind of horrible city was this? Karter shook his head in frustration. The pieces just didn't all quite fit together. How could one man be so evil? It made no sense. There had to be more to it. There just had to.

"Karter, which pile is the girl clothes?" Alick asked, bringing him back to reality. She was looking around, unable to see the going pile behind one of the trunks.

Karter pointed to the hidden pile where he'd been placing all the smaller dresses, and she smiled gratefully.

The clothes weren't in particularly good condition; there were holes in most of the articles and the colors were faded. But as each child exchanged their clothes from the blue course fabric pants and camouflage shirts to the styles of the kingdom, Karter had to admit they suddenly looked like normal villagers. They would blend into the crowd just fine. And apparently, that was a desired quality in this particular village.

Eventually, everyone was changed and had moved off to the campfire to talk amongst themselves. Everyone except Sam, Alick, Karter and Rydly.

"What's left?" Alick asked, sounding weary.

"Um... a handful of miscellaneous socks, some dresses, some trousers, a couple tunics..." Karter listed off, turning in a circle.

"These dresses are ridiculously ugly," Sam muttered, picking one up in disgust.

Alick rolled her eyes. "Wear it anyway, Sam," she said as if the argument was an old one.

Karter raised his eyebrows. If Sam refused, this could get interesting. But Sam just shrugged and picked up the darkest color gown she could find before disappearing into the trees to wash up.

"And make sure to get ALL the dirt out of your hair, Sam!" Alick yelled after her.

Karter looked back down at the clothes. The girls had it much easier; there was still a fair assortment of gowns and slippers to choose from. Karter was looking at three shirts and five pairs of pants—most of which looked too small.

"Can we just change our shirts?" he asked Rydly, bending over to find a pair of matching socks.

Rydly shook his head. "The blue color isn't found in the village. We would stick out."

"And why is that such a bad thing?"

"Anybody who's different in Conquistado is dead."

"I'm getting that." Karter blinked as that sunk in. What was wrong with this Fallon fellow? His kingdom wasn't a civilization, it was a death camp. "Why isn't the blue color found in the village? It must be easy to get if you guys use it."

"It was a color reserved for royalty until Fallon. The only way to get it is to crush up the berries grown deep in the forest. Since we've taken over the woods, Fallon's men have been unable to harvest them. It's quite ironic, really; we're dressed in the color of kings." Rydly smirked.

"Here, I think these will fit."

Karter looked up as Alick handed him a pile of clothing.

"Um...thanks," he muttered, a blush forming in his cheeks. Before she could notice, he turned and walked quickly away, ignoring Rydly's stare.

The ground crunched beneath his feet as he walked a little ways into the forest, where the light sparkled off the dew drenched leaves. Soon, once he'd assured himself he was out of view, instead of the blue pants and a camo shirt that Rydly had lent him, Karter was dressed in beige pants, an itchy, dark brown tunic and flimsy footwear.

The clothes were hole-free and looked new-ish, but Karter didn't think they looked *nice.* Weren't they supposed to look nice for this ceremony? Confused, he came back into camp and realized that all the older guys were dressed in similarly simple outfits.

"How strange," Karter muttered walking back out into the clearing. For a moment, he just stood there, unable to find Alick or Rydly.

Finally, spotting them by the fire circle, he walked toward them, realizing why he'd overlooked them at first. Alick had apparently visited the stream and her previously dirty and messy hair was damp and straight, occasionally showering water over her simple brown gown. Rydly, meanwhile, was in a very similar outfit to Karter's, his shirt just a little lighter. Sitting next to them was a third Pantasma that Karter didn't recall ever seeing before.

Curious, Karter drew up next to the group and then stumbled back a step as he realized that the third person was none other than Sam. Her once dirt speckled cheeks were now blemish-free and her hair was bright blonde, despite being soaking wet, and pulled up as gracefully as it could be so it covered her neck in little swirls. Sam's hair had had so much muck in it the day before he hadn't realized it was a lighter shade than Alick's.

Alick caught sight of Karter and smiled.

"Smashing," she said. "Now we can leave. Karter, stick with Rydly. Peter, start moving out!" she cried as she and Sam moved off into the crowd.

"You okay?" Rydly asked.

Karter shrugged. He wasn't sure he'd ever quite understand this way of life. "Why are our outfits so simple, but the young boys are so complicated?"

Rydly smiled. "To blend. All the men in the crowd will be from the construction project outside of town. They won't be wearing fancy clothes."

"The wall, you mean?"

"Yeah."

Karter followed Rydly through the crowd until they were situated at the back of the mass with Alick. There were an incredible number of them.

"So, Karter, what do you think of the camp?" Alick asked as they made their way through the thick forest.

"It's effective. And busy." Karter answered honestly. He still wasn't used to be given such attention from a leader. He was used to being ignored by power.

Alick let out a short laugh. "Well, we try our best," she murmured. "Bet this is a lot different than where you came from."

Karter nodded. "Definitely. In my kingdom the most of citizens were well off, happy, and cheerful." *I miss it*, Karter thought. Though even as he described the people, it sounded cliche. *I guess not everyone was well-off... But certainly more people than in this kingdom.*

A wistful expression danced across Alick's face so quickly, Karter wondered if he had imagined it.

"It's been a long time since this area has been cheerful," she whispered.

Karter was struck by the sudden urge to go and hug her. He couldn't imagine living for ten years as an outcast with no parents, no authority, and the responsibilities of a ruler. Because that's what Alick was. She was the queen of her own little society. The stress that was probably put on her would drive anyone else insane.

What seemed like an eternity later, the group reached the edge of the woods—the sun blindingly bright without the dense foliage filtering the rays. As Karter peered around the group, he saw that they were walking toward a dirt road filled with people traveling toward the city center. Did no one actually live there?

"Um, how exactly does Heritor Day produce an heir to the throne?" Karter asked, turning his attention back to the reason they were making this excursion.

"It's a lottery," Alick replied with a sigh. "They draw a name from a barrel."

"'Cause that's the best way to pick royalty," Sam muttered behind them.

Alick gave a short laugh and then continued. "If the King and Queen do not accept the person selected, that person has to fight for the kingdom."

"Wait, fight as in... go to war?" Karter asked, his eyes bugging out of his head slightly.

Rydly, Sam, and Alick nodded.

"The person selected has two choices, to accept the crown, or decline it," Rydly said.

"If they accept, but the King declines... we're at war. If they decline, we're back to square one and this ceremony is performed again in two years," Sam said. "It's a messed up design."

Karter looked at the three of them carefully. "What happened two years ago?" he asked.

Alick bit her lip and looked down. "The person selected was a widowed old woman. She declined. Like most everybody else for the past ten years."

"Why does nobody accept?" Karter asked.

"Fallon is not the kind of man to allow a random peasant to take over for him. He will never accept the selected person," Rydly sighed.

"So...?" Karter asked, "Why don't they just fight? Seems like a great chance for a rebellion if you ask me."

"So..." Sam continued slightly sarcastically. "Nobody wants to go against Fallon in a war. They'd be slaughtered. Fallon's smart. All the men are gone, so there's no way to form an opposing army."

"Then what is the point of continuing to have Heritor Day? And couldn't you use women?" Karter asked, getting annoyed at the inefficiency of the kingdom. They had too many problems and not one solution.

Sam, Alick, and Rydly looked at each other before Alick spoke up. "The youngest woman in the village is easily over thirty and none of them have ever been trained to fight. They have no will to either. Even in the Pantasmas, most of the girls would rather take care of camp than go on a suicide mission."

"And the boys will go on a suicide mission?"

Alick smirked. "I guess not willingly. All the Pantasmas would if I asked them to, but I don't. In a war against Fallon, we'd never stand a chance."

Karter had to agree with that. A small band of kids would never be able to compete against an army. Even if they did teach the villagers to fight, which would probably be too difficult anyway.

"So why is Heritor Day continued? There isn't a point."

"Some things are so ancient, not even Fallon can overrule them," Alick sighed. "Heritor Day isn't simply a tradition, Karter, it's a custom put in place by an ancient witch. To break the custom is to bring upon this kingdom a terrible curse." Alick continued. "Besides that, I think Fallon's hoping that one of these days a small boy will win, someone he can groom to be the perfect successor."

Karter shuddered. Even imagining such a corrupt man raising a child was frightening.

The group reached the road and began merging into the procession of people as they trudged resignedly toward the useless ceremony. Karter watched as Alick and Sam wove their way between people, blending in with an ease that seemed to indicate it was not uncommon for them to go to market day.

Karter couldn't help that Alick's hair had completely dried now and was hanging in gentle waves down her back. Sam's hair too, had dried, and Karter was right, it was blonder than Alick's.

Karter stumbled as Rydly pushed him from behind, and Karter was forced to watch where he put his feet. When he looked up again, the girls had disappeared.

"Come on," Rydly said, pushing him gently. "We have to hurry. It's almost time."

Karter nodded and picked up the pace, merging with the crowd from the forest and trying not to get crushed in the masses. By the time the town was visible, the crowd was so large that there was no moving forward.

"Around the edges," Rydly said quietly, forcing his way through the stopped crowd. As they made their way, they stuck close to buildings where the crowd was lessened, drawing closer to the castle with every footstep.

"Why are we going so close?" Karter asked.

"Battle strategy. Our places are just up ahead."

"I thought we weren't fighters."

Rydly turned around and handed Karter a dagger from within his shirt.

"This close to Fallon, everyone's a fighter." Rydly said in a low voice, looking around to make sure the soldiers ringing the crowd were looking the other way.

Karter took the dagger and gulped nervously, stowing it in his belt. He was about to ask what to watch for when a voice boomed out over the crowd.

"All hail Derex Fallon, King of Conquistado!"

Up above the crowd, on a balcony bedecked in flags, stood a single man in a simple page uniform reading aloud from a lengthy yellowing scroll.

"Karter, kneel now!" Rydly hissed. Karter looked around and saw he was the only one still standing. Whoops.

A fleet of trumpets heralded a second figure onto the balcony and he emerged, cloaked, his hands raised to welcome his people. The figure lowered his hood, and Karter saw a relatively large man with graying hair and a sneer that could kill. Even from this distance, Karter felt as if his eyes were scanning every inch of his soul.

"That's Fallon?" Karter whispered to Rydly.

Rydly glanced up and nodded.

Fallon nodded toward an old man with a large, pointed hat, probably the kingdom's priest, who began to read from a long scroll.

"In the event that no heir to the throne is willing or able to don the crown, or in the event that no heir exists, a drawing shall be held once every two years to obtain a new bloodline by decree of the Witch of Sombras." the priest read, his voice cracking slightly in his old age. "If the heir chosen does not wish to rule, they may object to the decree. If the current ruler does not approve of the chosen, a period of one year is given for the chosen to prove their worth in battle. If the chosen succeeds in removing the life from the monarch, they win the crown."

The priest stopped talking, and the crowd watched with bated breath as a large barrel was brought out from the castle.

"In this barrel, lie the names of every citizen in the great nation of Conquistado. If your name is drawn," the priest said ominously, "please proceed to the castle gate."

The tension of the town was palpable as the piece of paper was selected agonizingly slowly. Karter clenched his jaw; despite the useless nature of the ceremony, it was still surprisingly stressful. Simply the idea of having to go up so close to the malevolent man was enough to make one's hair stand on end.

"And the chosen heir is," the priest began, taking his time reading of the name of the unfortunate soul, "Alick Karenza Daven—" the priest cut off suddenly as Fallon pushed him aside and took the piece of paper.

The crowd was murmuring in rushed voices, "Daven?" "Did he mean Daveney?" "Is it possible?"

Karter's heart began racing. *Alick? Pantasma Alick?* This wasn't good. This wasn't good at all. She was public enemy number one! She couldn't go up there. Surely it was a common name in Conquistado.

"Well, well, well," Fallon said icily as he looked down upon the paper. Karter shuddered. His voice was even creepier than his looks. Karter turned toward Rydly and saw that he'd gone paler then a ghost. Karter's heart nearly stopped beating all together. If Rydly was concerned that must mean it was his Alick. Pantasma Alick. The now absolutely dead Alick.

"Karenza Davenport, step forward," Derex Fallon said, an evil glint in his eye and a smug confidence in his voice. Karter watched as Alick stepped forward, going toward the gate. *Alick, don't do it,* Karter thought.

"Go!" Rydly whispered frantically in Karter's ear.

"What?" Karter looked back at him, confused.

"Go!" Rydly said, pushing him forward, closer to castle, muttering, "This is bad."

CHAPTER 6

eep down, Alick knew she was being stupid. She was Alick Karenza Daveney, the leader of the Pantasmas, a regular thorn in Derex Fallon's side. And she was walking right into his own home!

He didn't even have the decency to say her name in front of the crowd. Though Alick couldn't say she blamed him. If the citizens knew who Alick really was, then all hell would break loose in Conquistado. For a second, however, she had wondered if Fallon would let the priest continue, actually say her name. Risk everything just to do the right thing. She should've known it was too good to be true. The almighty Derex Fallon would never allow it. He wouldn't allow anything that threatened his reign.

"Alick! Alick, stop!" Sam had managed to push her way through the crowd after her friend. There were probably several bruises involved. "Alick, this is suicide."

"Sam, when have we ever let that stop us?" Alick murmured.

"The crowd has figured out it's you, you know."

"What?!" Alick whipped around, suddenly scared. Fallon might let the leader of the Pantasmas try to fight to prove he was all powerful. But he would never let *her* fight. Her survival right now depended on the crowd *not* knowing the truth.

"Leader of the Pantasmas, you," Sam clarified. "The crowd has figured out that you lead our band of thieves."

"Your point?" Alick asked, continuing through the crowd toward the castle gate. Above her, she could feel Fallon's eyes watching her every move.

"Alick, you'll never make it out of there alive, and you know it!"

Alick whipped around again. "Sam, this is something I have to do. It's law. It's why we came."

"That was before we knew your name was going to come out of that barrel!"

"Sam, I'm going into that castle."

"Alick, please." Sam was desperate now, her normal sarcastic front was gone, and she was begging Alick.

"Sam, I'll be fine," Alick said with more confidence than she felt. Her insides felt like mush, but she pushed through the crowd and found herself in the last place she wanted to be, right in front of the palace gate. The gilt work was patchy, tackier than she remembered.

Swallowing audibly, Alick gathered all of her courage and stepped under the now-raised steel portcullis. As she did, Alick grimaced, remembering how before Fallon, the portcullis had been a simple wrought-iron gate, intricately carved and stronger than it looked.

I wonder how else Fallon's redecorated, she thought wryly, trying to calm her racing heart. It's a little known secret that shallow thoughts can keep the mind and heart at rest in times of overwhelming turmoil.

The castle hadn't changed at all. In ten years, the only differences were no-longer ivy-covered walls and a statue of Fallon in the middle of the walk. A statue built by the man, for the man. How stuck up could one get?

Alick looked up at the domes and towers and the wall, all of which seemed endless from her lowly position in the courtyard. The glorious arched windows gleamed brightly in the sunlight, the painted mosaics bright and cheerful as ever as they sat high and aloof in the recesses near the roof. It made Alick strangely nostalgic.

"So you did come."

Alick jumped as a figure came out from behind the statue. Alick recognized the balding man who seemed as unchanged as the castle.

"You scared me," Alick said, narrowing her eyes slightly.

"Ten years, Alick, you'd think some of your petty behaviors would have evaporated in the woods."

Alick shook her head. "Ten years, you'd think you'd have missed me," she retorted. Loque had been the castle butler since before she was even born. Part of her though he always would be.

Alick took a deep breath and walked past him toward the large castle door. She wanted this to be over with.

"Now hold up a minute! You're not actually going up there, are you?!"

"Well, that was the plan."

"Alick, you were lucky to escape this castle during the massacre ten years ago! You've been careful not to come within eyeshot of this place since. Why would you walk right up next to the man who wants your head on a platter?!"

"He won't hurt me in front of all these people, Loque." Alick said calmly, pushing her emotions deep inside until they were ineffective.

"Won't he?!" The old man was frantic. What was left of his pepper gray hair stuck up in all directions and wobbled as he limped quickly after Alick. That was one thing Alick always remembered about the old butler. He limped. Not once had she asked him why, but now she was curious.

"No Loque, he won't. It's Heritor Day, and I'm the chosen heir."

"Even more reason to dispose of you!"

"But that's not how Heritor Day works, now is it?" Alick replied with a sly grin. She wondered how she could keep convincing everybody else that it was fine when her own stomach was practically doing backflips.

"Alick," Loque said in a warning tone as she opened up the castle door.

"Loque, Fallon isn't stupid. The crowd out there knows I lead the Pantasmas. I'm a symbol to them. He'll reject me, sure, but only because he wants what everybody else in this godforsaken place wants."

"And what is that Alick?"

"He wants me to attack him."

"So what if he does? No one can attack Fallon, Alick. This debacle will be the death of you yet! "

"I've made my decision, Loque. Now come on, His Majesty doesn't like to be kept waiting." Alick set her resolve and climbed the stairs. Fallon was the source of her worst fears. If she could stand up to him, she could stand up to anything.

Though as she rounded the last bend in the staircase, Alick couldn't help but wonder: was she was really being brave? Or was she just being stupid like everyone seemed to think? She had long ago learned that bravery to prove a point rarely ends well.

Well, she thought as she came to the door, *too late now.*

CHAPTER 7

"Why hasn't she appeared yet?" Rydly demanded. Again.

"I keep telling you, Rydly, if that castle is as big as I think it is, it's going to take Alick a while to make her way up there."

"What if she's already dead?"

"If what you have told me about Fallon is true, if he's going to kill her for insubordination, he'll kill her in front of everybody as an example, and he'll do it himself," Karter reassured Rydly. But internally, Rydly's anxiety was rubbing off on him. Karter had been raised on stories of takeovers and political schemes. It wasn't difficult to imagine the worst.

In an attempt to distract Rydly and assuage his own nerves, Karter asked, "So why did Fallon call Alick by her middle name the second time?"

Rydly's head shot up and his eyes widened into the look of a cornered animal. "What?" he asked, too brightly.

"Why did Fallon call for Karenza Davenport the second time, and Alick Karenza Davenport the first time?"

"Um, in our society the middle name is kind of like what you go by in public. Elders call you by it, and any official document is signed with it."

Karter raised his eyebrows. "In my kingdom it was the opposite," he blurted out before he realized what he was saying.

Rydly looked at him surprised. "Huh. I suppose that makes more sense, actually."

Karter nodded slowly. He hadn't meant to give that away. He didn't want anyone knowing where he came from or who he was, and he knew what question was coming next: 'What is your first name?'. That was not a question he was willing to answer. Not yet.

"So what's your "proper" name?" Karter asked before Rydly could pry further.

"Aaron."

"What about Sam?" Karter asked, still trying to postpone the inevitable question.

Rydly smiled wickedly. "Krisalyn. Her name is Samantha Krisalyn—she's up!"

Karter jerked his head up and saw Alick next to Fallon. His blood ran cold as all Rydly's worries rushed back into Karter's head like the tide.

"Why are we just standing here?" Karter whispered frantically. "We need to help her!"

Rydly raised his eyebrows at Karter's sudden concern. "We are in a good position." He muttered, fingering a knife-like lump in his pocket.

Karter looked around, wondering if he'd missed something strategic about their location. They were still by the empty alley in a crowd of people, thirty feet from the gate and nearly fifty from Fallon. "How? We can't do any good from here."

Rydly looked pained. "We're not supposed to be here at all," he said. "If something went wrong, which it did, you and I were supposed to retreat with most of the Pantasmas. The warriors were to handle everything."

"Then why are we still here?"

"I'm not going to hear the fate of my friend second-hand," Rydly muttered darkly.

Karter grimaced. *Get out of there, Alick*, he thought frantically. Fallon's right hand was no place for rebel leader. And if it went south there was no way to help her.

CHAPTER 7

CHAPTER 8

arely had Alick felt as terrified as she did when she walked out onto the balcony with Derex Fallon, the murderer himself. Alick still remembered that night: the screaming, the blood, the weeks of hiding in the cellar before her escape to the woods.

She still remembered his cold, penetrating eyes. The eyes that were looking right at her, right now.

"Well, if it isn't our little Karenza," he drawled, the cordial tone laced with icy fire that pierced Alick with every word.

Alick swallowed and tried to summon enough courage to speak. She was no longer the child Fallon remembered who could barely color in the lines. She was a woman, a leader, and every bit a match for him.

"Is our little rebel too scared to speak?"

Alick grit her teeth. "Never," she spat.

"No need to be testy. This is an auspicious occasion." Fallon stared her down.

"Then get on with it," Alick said, her stomach threatening to disgorge what little she had eaten that morning. It was a risk to mouth off to him even on a good day.

Fallon raised a single, pointed eyebrow toward the priest, but never stopped looking at Alick. It was as if he was calculating her soul. Alick remembered that look from her childhood.

Even then he had creeped her out.

"Please welcome the chosen, Alick Karenza!" The priest cried to the crowd. Alick walked forward with her head held high. The crowd was silent, then as they saw exactly who she was, recognized her from the wanted posters, they all began cheering. It had been too long, and Alick still stood too far away, for the crowd to realize how much Alick looked like her mother. And the page still had never told the crowd her real last name: Daveney. The name that every child was taught from birth. It had been an awfully long time since she'd heard it.

Fallon and the priest stepped forward, the priest next to Alick and Fallon on his other side. Alick briefly wondered where his wife, Kana, was.

"Do you, Derex Fallon, King of Conquistado, accept the drawing that has been made this day?" the priest asked, nervously sweating, expecting, like Alick, for something unexpected to happen at any second. Like a beheading.

For a moment, Alick even wondered if Fallon would say "yes".

"Never." No such luck.

One word. One word that suddenly put a whole lot more pressure on Alick.

"Do you, Karenza Daven—" Fallon brought his foot down hard on top of the priest's before he could finish. "port!" the priest gasped in pain and then he started over. "Do you, Karenza Davenport, chosen of Heritor Day, accept that you are now opposed?" The poor priest was shaking now.

Alick swallowed loudly again. "Yes," she said definitively. "I accept that I am opposed." The crowd began to murmur. Probably wondering if she was sane. It was a fair question, really.

"Do you accept the terms of war and agree to fight for this kingdom and the crown as a way to defeat this opposition?"

The crowd silenced itself. Someone dropped a pin and the sound clattered like a gunshot. Alick thought about the choice she was being given. She could overthrow Fallon, become the Queen, and have a chance to restore the kingdom to its former glory.

But she had no army, just followers, friends. Kids. They were all just kids. Saying yes was about the stupidest thing to do. It was suicide. And yet... Alick looked out over the crowd and managed to find Sam, right where she was supposed to be. Twenty feet behind her, Rydly and Karter stood by an ally. The sight of the three of them lifted Alick up and gave her the courage to say the unthinkable.

"I do," Alick proclaimed.

And as the crowd cheered, Fallon's icy eyes found hers. "Don't think you can ever get back what was yours."

"Watch me," Alick replied, turning and darting down the stairs before he could retaliate. The full enormity of what she'd just done crushing her as she stood concealed in the stone stairway. Nothing would be the same now. *Please let it be for the better.*

CHAPTER 9

If Karter had known ahead of time that Alick was going to win the lottery to become Queen, and then accept the challenge, immediately plunging the little band of thieves into a war that they couldn't win against an insane demonic ruler... Karter would definitely have heeded Kaernon's warning to stay away.

If only his parents had known of this suicide town, perhaps they'd have given him a freaking map. Or maybe they had known this was the closest town to theirs and just wanted him out of the way. That was a scary thought.

The end of the ceremony had been an uneventful one. Alick had walked out of the palace unscathed, and the Pantasmas still in the crowd had walked her back to camp like an honor guard. Nobody had seen her since.

"Ow!" Karter cried out. He looked back down at the log he was de-barking and smacked the bug that had bit him.

He looked over at Rydly and pursed his lips.

"How have you all survived out here in the wilderness for so long?" Karter exclaimed. "No running water, all these bugs, making absolutely everything from scratch..."

"Well, first off, only the palace has running water. Second, you get used to the bugs after a while. Third, we don't make *everything* from scratch. We're not called a band of thieves for nothing." Karter noted the bitterness in Rydly's last words and wondered if there was a story he was missing.

"So you guys actually steal stuff?"

Rydly grimaced but he nodded. "We try to only take from Fallon. But sometimes we don't have a choice in the matter."

"How can you not have a choice?" Karter asked, not comprehending.

"Well I suppose life or death *is* a choice..." Rydly trailed off.

Karter was horrified.

"Riddle! Carrot! Aren't you two done with that bark yet?"

"Is she always so—"

"Yes," Rydly answered dully. "We're doing our best, Slime."

Karter raised his eyebrows at Rydly's attempt to insult Sam. He needed lessons in comebacks. Luckily, Karter was quite adept at them after growing up with so many siblings.

"Just work faster," Sam spat. "We're all waiting on you."

"Waiting for what?" Karter asked.

"Apparently training efforts are doubling. Everyone's learning to defend themselves, which means Riddle has to get his hands dirty." Sam stalked off, cutting off a tree limb with her sword on her way.

"We get to learn to fight?" Karter clarified.

Rydly looked like someone had slapped him for no reason. "It would seem so," he said, giving Karter an incredulous look.

Karter smiled. "Then let's get crackin'!"

"Due to recent... events," Peter began, shooting Alick a pained look.

Karter's eyes narrowed. He felt Rydly's hand on his arm and realized he'd taken a step forward. Peter hadn't noticed, but Alick had. Karter felt her eyes on him as he backed up again, so he was in line with the others. Peter was the epitome of bullies and it grated on his nerves. Maybe it was just because he reminded him of his elder brother, but whenever Peter talked, Karter got an urge to punch him in the mouth.

"We find it necessary to train each and every one of you, not just our warriors. If you have fought with us before, step to the right. If you haven't, step to the left."

Karter and Rydly stepped to the left along with most of the children and a few of the older girls. It was mildly embarrassing. Karter wished, probably for the thousandth time, that he'd been the non-banished twin. Peter walked over to the right and began giving them more detailed orders while Alick came over to the left.

"So," she said. "Who's ready to learn?"

Rule number one of the Pantasmas: Don't piss Sam off.

Rule number two of the Pantasmas: Never let Alick teach you sword fighting. Ever.

Karter lay on the ground, leaves sticking to his clothes, feeling rather as if he'd run into a tree. Alick had beaten him. Again. At least he was doing better than Rydly, who was paired with a girl named Skye. She was five feet of vicious when you gave her a sword.

"Karter, come on. Try again," Alick told him. Again. He wondered if she enjoyed using him as a punching bag.

"You know getting consistently knocked to the ground is not making me want to get up again," Karter snapped, letting his head rest on the hard, leaf strewn soil, enjoying the few moments of respite.

Alick laughed. "So you never tried to be a knight for your kingdom?" she asked, hauling him to his feet.

Karter winced. "My parents were never exactly... supportive of me. I was a sickly child." Karter kept his eyes down, refusing to look at Alick. He felt her eyes scanning him, looking at him with curiosity, but she wasn't Sam. She respected people. And she didn't ask any more questions.

"Well, you're not sickly anymore. So hold your blade up high. Let's try again."

Karter moaned and held his blade parallel to the ground, facing Alick.

"Remember to keep your feet apart. You want to stay balanced. Keep your blade up. Don't look down! Keep your wrist steady. Strength comes from your weight shifting, not your muscles." And on. And on. And on.

As Karter and Alick fought, she tried to tell him what was wrong, what was right, how to stand, how to jab. It was too much for him to handle, and soon, Karter was once again on the forest floor.

"You okay?" Alick asked, sounding thoroughly unconcerned.

Karter glared at her from the ground. Here she was, in a dress, barely a hair out of place, with no visible perspiration; meanwhile, Karter was sure he looked worse than when he had been traveling. His hair was stiff and his clothes were drenched with sweat. Leaves and dirt clung stuck wherever they could, and he was bleeding in several places.

He was clearly *not* okay. And he was definitely *not* good at sword-fighting.

Alick took in his appearance and bit her lip. She looked around at the others and then sighed.

"I guess we should call it a day."

Karter's eyebrows shot up in surprise. Then he looked around and saw that everybody else had started going about their usual duties again. He turned back around to Alick and glared at her again, getting up off the ground.

He took a step toward the camp, and fell flat on his face.

Behind him, he heard Alick trying her best not to laugh as she came and knelt next to him.

"Are you okay?" she asked, sounding both amused and concerned.

"I'm fine," Karter grumbled, sitting up and looking over to where he had tripped to see the source. It was his sword. Go figure.

Karter shut his eyes and let his head fall.

"I'm horrible," he muttered.

"You're not *that* bad," Alick said.

Karter pursed his lips. "I just tripped over my own sword."

"Yes, but you are dead tired and can barely walk at all, so really, it's not as bad as it sounds."

Karter looked at Alick like she was crazy, but she simply shrugged and stood up, offering him her hand.

"So how did you learn how to sword fight?" Karter asked as she hauled him up. He retrieved his sword from the ground before he could trip over it again and wiped sweat from his brow.

Alick cocked her head to one side. "What do you mean?"

"Well, knights are always guys." Karter began. "The only girls I've seen trained in combat were archers. Plus, you've been in the woods for a decade. Nobody I've ever known was trained in sword fighting before age ten, and you weren't even that old yet."

Alick shrugged. "Well, you certainly have valid points."

"That's not an answer," Karter grumbled.

"We taught ourselves, mostly."

Karter's jaw dropped. "You learned to be that good by yourself?" he asked, disbelieving.

Alick nodded. Why was this girl so much cooler than he was?

"Why didn't you teach Rydly before now?" Karter asked, changing the subject.

Alick smiled mischievously. "Who says we didn't teach him anything?"

Rule number three of the Pantasmas: When Alick becomes cryptic, run in the opposite direction. For a level-headed leader, she had a dangerous streak.

"Shh," Alick hissed.

"There is nothing to hear us!" Karter exclaimed. He, Rydly, and Alick had been crawling in the underbrush for a really long time, and Karter was getting annoyed. His knees were starting to hurt, and his cuts were opening up again. Even if someone *was* near enough to hear them, they could just track the blood stains instead.

Alick turned around and made sure he saw her rolling her eyes. Fine, he was whiny. But seriously! What on earth were they doing sneaking through bushes in the middle of a deserted forest? It was *deserted*.

"Okay, we're here. Rydly, you can do the honors."

"What, why me?"

"Karter wants to see your skill."

"Um," Karter put in. "I don't know what we're talking about."

Rydly shook his head. "All right, on three."

Karter still had no idea what was going on. Why were they counting?

"One," Alick said, crouching as if ready to spring.

"Two," Rydly followed, producing a bow and quiver from who knows where.

The two looked over at Karter expectantly.

"Uh, three?"

It was as if he had fired a shot. Rydly and Alick burst out of the underbrush and took off toward something.

Karter stood up slowly, still not sure what was happening, just in time to see Rydly fire three successive shots at Alick who was busy sprinting in zig zags.

Each arrow hit its mark.

"WHY DID YOU SHOOT ALICK?!" Karter yelled, rushing over to the fallen girl.

Who was sitting up. Laughing.

Karter furrowed his eyebrows. On Alick's arm was a shield with a bulls-eye painted on it. All three arrows were embedded squarely in the middle of the bulls-eye. Three perfect shots.

"You shot three bulls-eyes at a moving target?" Karter turned and asked Rydly, clearly impressed, but still annoyed no one had warned him.

Rydly nodded. "Um, yeah. Almost every Pantasma can do it." He shrugged his shoulders like it was no big deal.

Karter's jaw dropped, which of course just made Alick laugh harder. Honestly, Karter didn't understand what was so funny about the whole situation. Then again, he didn't understand much about this kingdom. Perhaps the two were related.

"So that's what you meant earlier, before this whole expedition. That's what you taught Rydly: how to shoot." *Why couldn't you have just told me that?* Karter screamed in his head.

Alick nodded, smiling wide. "Weapons of thieves. We're experts."

Karter noted that Alick seemed almost proud of that fact. Either that or it was some sort of inside joke he was missing.

"So...am I supposed to learn?" Karter asked. He wasn't sure he wanted to try shooting at live targets. What if he missed the target?

Alick shrugged. "Maybe later," she said. "Shooter takes lots of practice."

"Shooter?"

"The game we just played."

"You play that as a *game*?" Karter exclaimed.

"Yes," Alick answered like that was the obvious answer.

"But it's dangerous!"

Rydly laughed. "Dude, you've got a lot to learn."

"I'm getting that," Karter grumbled. "So, when do I start?" he asked. He had made up his mind. All of his life he'd been weak and useless, and here it was no different. But that was going to change. He wasn't going to rest until he could pull his own weight.

"Patience," Alick replied. "All good things come in time."

CHAPTER 10

"Quiet!" Alick practically screamed as she reentered camp. All around her, the hubbub finally stilled. "What is going on?" she asked, completely confused and more than a little panicked. The entire band of Pantasmas was stocked to the teeth with weapons ranging from real swords to twigs the children collected.

"Fallon has his armies stationed on Juliet's farm!" Peter proclaimed. "The ones who are truly loyal to him. Our scouts report they are watching all the roads going in and out of the forest."

"Idiots," Sam snorted. "Don't they know we avoid the roads?"

Alick shot Sam a glare that clearly read *not helping*.

"What exactly were you planning to do about it?" Alick asked Peter, her voice conveying the warning in her words. How dare he organize the entire Pantasmas with zero strategy, giving even little Sally a weapon.

Yes, Juliet was an important asset for the Pantasmas, but there was no need to send in the toddlers.

"Um...wait for your orders," Peter replied carefully.

"Good," Alick said testily. Then she called out, "If you are not normally in our strike force, return to work. The rest of you, in position."

"Alick."

Alick turned as Rydly called her name. She saw the silent plea in his eyes and grimaced. Rydly was not part of the strike force, but he was very handy in a raid, and she *had* promised him some more action. Since he'd hit puberty, Rydly was no longer the wimpy string bean he had been growing up in the woods.

"All right, you can come," Alick ventured. "But you have to bring Karter. It's your job to show him the ropes." Alick turned back before Rydly could process what she said. She didn't want to see the indignation that might appear. Rydly had been a Pantasma since the beginning and had only begun coming on raids in the past year. Karter had been in the camp for a very short while, was currently much less competent with a weapon, and yet Alick was allowing him to come. If Rydly was a prideful person, Alick knew that this would be a blow. Luckily for her, though, Rydly was a very forgiving person.

Why am *I letting Karter come?* Alick wondered to herself. She couldn't seem to settle on an answer.

Alick walked through the camp to her tent, mindful of her warriors scurrying about and preparing to deliver a decisive blow to the enemy. Alick couldn't help but wonder what Fallon's motives were for sticking an army outside the forest.

Surely it wasn't coincidence that he had taken up residence on the farm that was the kindest to the Pantasmas. Was Alick leading her warriors into a trap?

"Why are we bringing Riddle and the newbie along?" Sam asked curiously, yanking Alick out of her thoughts.

"Good practice," Alick murmured.

Sam raised her eyebrows. "So what's the plan? We've never struck Juliet's place before. She normally just gives us what we need."

Alick sighed heavily. Her mind felt so full of apprehension and responsibility that she was surprised it hadn't burst. Normally she had days to plan these things, to think through every combination.

"I don't know, Sam. Why does Fallon even have his armies there? What if it's a trap?"

"Alick, Fallon is just trying to throw you off your game and, by the looks of things, its working."

Alick tried to defend herself, but Sam cut her off and continued, "Alick, Fallon has controlled and ruined our lives and the villager's lives for a decade. Now is our chance to stop him, to get rid of him. If we get destroyed in the process, at least we will have tried."

Alick was silent.

"Now," Sam said, "what's the plan?"

"When did you become so on board with this whole overthrowing the King business?"

Sam rolled her eyes. "You're avoiding my question."

"We'll rain havoc from the trees with archers, use the edges of the forest to our advantage, and make them come to us." Alick listed off, almost automatically. It was one of the oldest tricks they used.

"What if they just shoot back? These are Fallon's men; they know the forest is our terrain and are unlikely to come closer." Sam sought for flaws in the plan so that they could be sealed tight.

"Then we send a strike team around to drive them toward us. It can't be too different from our siege of the wall last year." Alick rubbed her head to try and assuage the growing headache.

"Except this time there are more soldiers and more is at stake."

"I thought you were supposed to be giving me a pep talk," Alick replied grumpily. "Not dissuading me from the plan."

Sam smirked. "Point taken. Now let's go. These soldiers are too close for comfort, and Juliet deserves better."

Alick jumped from tree to tree, her quiver slamming against her back, and twigs catching her hair and clothes with such frequency, Alick was surprised she wasn't yet in shreds. Below, above, and beside her, Alick could feel the tremors as her Pantasmas also made their way through the forest. Her attack force was made of about seventy individuals, nearly half the Pantasmas. Alick hoped that by the time she had to go up directly against Fallon, every Pantasma over the age of 12 would be ready to fight. But even then, they would be vastly outnumbered. They already were. Alick shook these thoughts from her head and plunged on until she could see the forests end.

Alick let out a sharp bird cry and heard all rustling cease as her Pantasmas obeyed the signal to stop. Alick let out a different, quieter bird call and Sam appeared, as if out of nowhere. Alick nodded to her once and watched as Sam dropped silently out of the tree to leave Rydly and his ground attackers a message.

The Pantasma's force was split into three. Alick led the tree crawlers, Peter led one ground crew and Rydly led the other ground crew. Sam considered this a horrible idea, but Alick needed Sam for the attack. She could not be spared to lead a ground team in Rydly's place.

As soon as Alick heard Sam swing back into the canopy of the trees, Alick let out a single long, whistling bird cry, the signal to move in.

Alick leapt to the next tree and swung herself through the branches like a monkey until she could clearly see Fallon's army laid out before her. Peter had been right; it was comprised of men loyal to Fallon: children that had been raised under Fallon's command in the castle, and men that had helped Fallon take the town.

In short, there was no one to show them mercy.

The sun disappeared below the horizon, and Alick let out one last loud whistle. The signal to attack.

As one, the Pantasmas dropped from the higher tree limbs to land on the lowest boughs or the ground, and let loose a stream of arrows toward the camp.

Alick launched herself out of the tree line and shot three arrows in quick succession; each one flaming high into the sky; the signal for the ground strike teams. Rydly would see the flaming arrows and begin his attack.

Shifting positions, Alick began shooting more arrows into the camp, aiming to seal shut the tents. She heard a few screams as the arrows found marks in arms reaching from the tents.

Alick grimaced. She was glad that the marks weren't heads. She hated killing. Alick continued loosing arrows, her goal to trap the knights for as long as possible. When she was confident enough time had passed for Rydly's group to be near, Alick moved in.

Darting expertly through the tents, Alick lit them on fire as she went, gathering weapons and food to the best of her ability on the way. On her back was a container for storing these items so she could keep her hands free as needed. A sword flashed in Alick's peripheral vision, and she ducked in time to avoid getting sliced by the knight cutting himself out of his tent. Alick backpedalled and ran back the way she'd come before the man saw her. Leaning against a pole, she sighed in relief. This part of the mission relied on stealth, not confrontation. Weapons were a necessity, and it would be much easier to steal them while the knights were preoccupied trying to fight off the Pantasmas. Elsewhere, Sam and a few key fighters were doing the same.

Moving on, Alick ducked into a newly vacated tent and grabbed a spear and a quiver of arrows that had been left behind. From outside, Alick heard the sound of running feet, and suddenly the air was full of shouts and thuds. It didn't take a genius to figure out what had happened. A ground strike team had arrived.

CHAPTER 11

nderneath the brush, Rydly's strike team waited with apprehension. Lit arrows flew into the sky, and Karter gasped audibly from panic and exhilaration.

"Time to move," Rydly said, shifting and standing up. The strike team followed suit, leaving Karter to scramble behind them. Karter had never seen Rydly act so authoritative, and he wondered if he was trying to prove something. Karter hurried and caught up to Rydly just as he ground to a stop, his eyes on the forest floor.

"What is it?" Karter asked.

"Shh," murmured Rydly. "It's around here somewhere."

Karter furrowed his eyebrows. What could possibly be on the ground that Rydly would be looking for? They were in the middle of a raid; it was no time for scavenger hunts.

"Here it is!" Rydly cried suddenly.

"What is?" Karter asked, slightly impatient.

"Orders," Rydly said simply. He stood and turned to the group, giving Karter a clear view of the "orders".

To Karter, it just looked like a bunch of lines forming an abstract shape.

"All right, men," Rydly began. "We're to storm in from the South corner, driving west. Show the mercy they will not show you."

The strike team grumbled at the last bit, but they swallowed their complaints and took off.

"You got all that from a bunch of squiggly lines?" Karter asked incredulously.

Rydly nodded. "It's symbol writing. All the Pantasmas can read and write at least a little bit of it. Sam's the best we have.

"She left you the message?"

Rydly nodded. "Very few of us can read and write, so symbols offer a good alternative."

"Isn't that harder? To learn countless symbols instead of the alphabet?"

Rydly shrugged. "Surprisingly not. But, then again, our symbol vocabulary is much smaller than that of a true language, and very few of us are completely fluent in them."

Karter let that digest. He had always been taught how to read and write. For him, it was these strange symbols that were the mystery.

"Rydly, who *can* read and write?"

"Um... Alick."

"That's it?" Karter asked.

"I think Sam can read some; Alick teaches her."

Karter was silent. He was stunned by the lack of education in the Pantasmas. Though the more Karter thought about it, the more sense it made. After all, Alick couldn't be expected to be a slave to their education when she was kept busy keeping the group safe from Fallon. But surely some of the older children should be able to read; they had memories from before Fallon's rule.

"Karter, all the nobles and their families were either killed or taken in by Fallon. None of the Pantasmas save Alick came from that society." Rydly continued as if he could read Karter's mind.

Karter nodded absently, his head still a whirl of thoughts.

He was shaken out of his reverie by the sounds of battle coming from up ahead. He and Rydly burst from the trees and were met by an onslaught of soldiers of both sides. Karter quickly drew his sword in time to block a strike aimed directly for his head. He was overwhelmed within moments forcing Rydly to come to his rescue.

"Come on!" Rydly yelled pulling Karter out of a pile up moments before he lost a limb. The two quickly backpedaled into the trees and climbed up into the branches. Karter watched the fighting from his vantage point and realized that he and Rydly were both hopelessly unskilled for a battle such as this.

"I thought this was supposed to be a raid," Karter shouted over the din.

Rydly grimaced. "It is," he shouted back. "This," he gestured to the battle where Fallon's soldiers were surrounded by a thin line of Pantasmas, "is simply a distraction."

"A mighty dangerous distraction," Karter murmured.

"It's a mighty dangerous raid. Not only do we want supplies, we want to injure enough of the army that they feel the need to find a new place to camp."

Karter watched as the battle started turning against the Pantasmas. Rydly let loose several arrows at once, severely wounding many of the enemy soldiers. Karter glimpsed a flash of blonde hair disappearing behind a tent in the distance, but couldn't see who it belonged to.

"I feel useless just sitting here in a tree," Karter said in frustration.

"Then we should work on our sword skills," Rydly replied, letting loose two more arrows.

Karter pursed his lips and returned his attention to the battle. He saw a figure in the distance slinking away with something clasped firmly in his hand.

Further from the figure was a dark shape on a hill holding a lantern. Karter didn't know what was going on but he knew whatever it was, he couldn't let the soldier reach the lantern. He'd sat in on enough battle strategy classes to recognize when something important was escaping.

Quick as a flash, he jumped from the tree and took off, skirting the battle the best he could whilst Rydly yelled at him from afar. Karter tuned it all out and focused his energy on the small, glowing point in the distance. Distantly, he wondered what exactly he was trying to stop.

If nothing else, Karter was fast. He may have been useless at sword fighting, unable to fire an arrow in a straight line, and a klutz when it came to day to day chores, but Karter could run. Sprinting over the rough terrain, Karter caught up to the knight in no time, reaching him just before he crested the last hill before his rendez-vous.

The soldier holding the lantern gave a shout and began running toward them.

Shoot, Karter thought. *There's no way I can take on two guys at once.* With this in mind, Karter quickly swept his sword across the back of his first foe's knees. The man crumpled to the ground with a loud thud and Karter scrambled to his hands, ripping what he was clutching away from him. Glancing down quickly, Karter saw that it was a necklace of some sort. *That's weird,* he thought before an arrow landed right between his feet.

Leaping into action, Karter whirled around with his sword up and ready, taking care to step on the arms of the fallen soldier. The man was more injured then he probably should have been because he had kept his hands clutched around the necklace instead of using them to break his fall.

The second foe finally reached Karter and, without hesitation, began his attack. The soldier fought viciously and quickly, forcing Karter to focus all his energy on blocking the attacks and staying alive. Luckily for Karter, his attacker was not as skilled as Alick or the men down in the camp, or his life would have been forfeited in mere minutes. As it was, he was clearly losing. His arms were criss-crossed with cuts, and the attacker just kept gaining the advantage.

As Karter was pressed back down the hill, he devoted more of his attention to keeping his balance than blocking the attacks. The attacker pressed this advantage and swung at Karter's arm.

Karter cried out in pain and clutched the bleeding gash. The duo had reached the bottom of the hill, and Karter was ready to drop from exhaustion. Down in the valley, light was so scarce, his enemy seemed to disappear for long periods of time before striking again, placing Karter in a state of constant panic as he attempted to gauge where the next attack would come from.

An arrow came racing down the hill, fired by the first foe still a top the hill. The point plunged into Karter's shoulder and he screamed.

With one arm incapacitated and the other trembling from the large gash and the weight of the sword, Karter looked up into the second soldier's face and knew that the end was coming.

The soldier grinned cruelly and spoke with contempt. "You are not worth killing," he muttered. With a stroke of mirth, he brought the hilt of his sword down upon Karter's head, and the world went dark. His last thought was that the second foe seemed curiously unconcerned about the trinket Karter had taken. Unless the attacker didn't realize that Karter had taken it.

CHAPTER 12

For such an intense raid, the losses were surprisingly few. However, they were still there, and each weighed heavily on Alick's heart. Two were dead, almost all were injured...and Karter was missing.

This last grievance weighed particularly heavy on Alick's heart. Part of her knew she shouldn't have sent him on the raid at all. He wasn't a warrior yet. The little solace Alick had came from the fact that Karter was only "missing." "Missing" could be found. "Missing" wasn't dead... not yet.

And so the search parties were scattered to the four winds to look for him, spies were sent to the village to eavesdrop, and informers from within the castle were pestered for any information regarding the night's antics.

"When are we doing the funeral rights for Bock and Eric?" Sam asked, coming up quietly behind Alick and sounding uncharacteristically somber.

Alick grimaced. "You know our policy. Nothing is final until all people are accounted for."

"He'll turn up, Alick. They always do."

"But what state will he turn up in?"

Sam grimaced. "Why him?"

"What do you mean, Sam?"

"I mean that Karter is not our first missing person. He's not one of the two guys who were killed last night! And yet it's Karter who is filling your mind. I have never seen you this stressed about a missing person, Alick. Not even when Rydly got lost for three days."

Alick closed her eyes. Everything Sam said was true. She couldn't dispute it.

"Sam... you see Karter just as I do. And you see the other Pantasmas. If a Pantasma is lost, they know how to take care of themselves. They know how to find their way back."

"And Karter's not a Pantasma," Sam concluded.

Alick shook her head, her stomach in knots. She had practically forced this life upon Karter. If something happened to any of the Pantasmas, Alick could always find a way to blame Fallon; that helped keep her sane. But there was no out this time. Karter's death would be her fault, plain and simple, and Alick wasn't sure she could live with that.

"I should never have let him leave camp, Sam."

Sam, instead of agreeing with Alick like she wanted to, showed what a true friend she was and shook her head "no."

"Alick, Karter was meant to go on this raid, or he wouldn't have been on it. You brought him along because you can see the good in people. You can see the warrior Karter can be, even if he isn't quite there yet."

Sam and Alick were silent for a long time before Sam finished. "Alick, you saw me for who I had the potential to be; that's something no one else in this camp sees to this day. They fear me. And I try hard to keep it that way. You see past that and you see past Karter. He'll be fine. And he will be the best warrior in the Pantasmas."

Alick smiled; she knew Sam didn't truly think Karter would ever be a warrior, but she appreciated it all the same. "Thanks, Sam," she whispered. "While we're on the subject of warriors, I would like you to train Rydly as a swordsman. He'll learn the fastest from you."

Sam made a face, but bit off her protests and instead asked why.

"Because, Sam, Rydly despises being inferior to you, and your constant bickering makes him excel far quicker then any other method I've tried. After all, you taught him archery," Alick said with a sly smile.

Sam stuck her tongue out. "Flatter my teaching skills all you want; it's not going to make me more willing to do this."

Alick managed a genuine laugh at this. "Thank you, Sam."

Sam smiled in return. "Meh, anytime."

"Alick, we have news of Karter!" Peter came bursting into the tent, his entrance hindered by a clothing trunk Peter promptly tripped over, sending him sprawling by Alick's feet.

"What's the news?" Alick asked impatiently as Peter lay on the floor groaning and Sam cracked up in the corner.

"Juliet has him. She sent a bird over the forest."

"What kind of bird?" Alick asked.

Peter shrugged as he picked himself off the floor. He was still trying to get back into Alick's good graces after organizing the Pantasmas without her the day before, and as a result had been hurrying more than he usually would. Served him right.

"You have got to me kidding me!" Sam exclaimed. "If you don't know what kind of bird it is, how do you know it wasn't a hawk from Fallon or a crow from town?"

"I know enough to know it wasn't either one of them. It wasn't black, and it didn't have a pointy head."

"A pointy head?! That's how you distinguish a hawk? You're ridiculous! Have Alick and I taught you nothing?"

"Hey, it works perfectly fine—"

"Guys!" Alick shouted, interrupting their argument. "It's probably worth checking out. Peter, stay here. Sam and I will go."

"But Alick—"

"I don't want to hear it, Peter. We're going. I don't care about the risk. Besides, I need to have a talk with Juliet." Alick pushed the tent flaps aside and strode across camp, not stopping to talk to anyone. No matter what anyone said, she still felt responsible for anything that happened to Karter. The other Pantasmas on the strike teams had chosen this life. Karter hadn't been afforded that luxury.

CHAPTER 13

Everything was quiet when Karter woke up staring at a thatch roof. Instead of the distant sounds of battle, the roar of a crackling fire was the only source of noise that penetrated the otherwise silent atmosphere. Confused, Karter tried to prop himself up on his elbows to look about, which was a huge mistake. Karter lay back down and groaned, trying to get his head to stop swimming nauseatingly. Vaguely, images of the night before began to trickle into his consciousness, and Karter remembered the hit he had taken to his head.

While waiting for the pounding in his head to subside, Karter began to take in more of his surroundings. He was lying on a stone floor— that much was clear. A blanket separated him from the cold flagstones, but Karter could still sense their shape.

A door opened and closed somewhere to his right, making Karter jump and causing his head to start pounding again.

"Ah, you're awake." A kind voice floated through the room.

Karter simply put a hand to his head to try and stop the incessant ache.

"Drink this," the voice murmured, leaning down and tipping a warm liquid into Karter's mouth.

Karter swallowed the liquid greedily. It tasted almost like honey, but was smooth as water and had an almost cinnamon aftertaste.

"That should help your head. You took quite the hit."

Karter's headache subsided enough to allow him to speak so he asked the question he had been dying to know the answer to.

"Where am I?"

"In my house, about a hundred feet from the valley where I found you. And it's a good thing I found you before Fallon's men did."

Karter blinked and managed to sit up. "Who are you?" he asked, getting a good look at the woman for the first time. She was on the younger side, definitely under 40, dressed in a simple brown dress and a cream apron. Her tawny hair was pulled back into a loose bun with wisps of it falling into her face.

"My name is Juliet. What's yours?"

"Karter," he murmured. "It was your farm that Fallon's men camped on."

Juliet nodded. "The greed they possess is almost inconceivable," she muttered. "They're always taking what they want when they want it. Children disappear to be trained as soldiers. Entire families are taken, split apart, and used in the castle. As maids, butlers, cooks..." As she talked, Juliet bustled around the kitchen, preparing a meal.

"What time is it?"

"Nearly supper. I suspect someone will be along to fetch you soon. They normally appear around dusk."

"They?" Karter asked cautiously.

Juliet smiled. "The Pantasmas. I assume you came from them. You weren't dressed like the knights.

"You know, my children live among the Pantasmas. I did too for a while. Fallon found out I was pregnant. Any new children born are supposed to be handed over to the castle to be raised there. I knew I could never let him get my children, so when his men came, I ran. My husband was away, working on that godforsaken wall.

"Alick found me. She let me stay with them until Ashton and Ashley were four. By then they had enough other help to take care of the children..." she trailed off for a moment before adding, "and it was no place for me."

"But they were your children. Why didn't you stay?"

"The Pantasma's camp is no place for a grown-up like me." Juliet chuckled. "To live with them, you must be useful to them. And I was becoming a hindrance. Too motherly for their ragtag bunch. Too big to hide well. Though I suppose by now they've solved that problem..." she trailed off again.

Karter lowered his head and thought about what she'd said. Was he useful? He couldn't be. After all, he couldn't fight, he couldn't shoot, he couldn't track. He wasn't even good at the stuff Rydly did, like cooking or building a fire. He was a guy who cared for lost animals, who let his brother bully him as long as it kept his other siblings safe, who never explored or did anything wrong because he couldn't stand causing his mother any more pain than he did simply for existing. Would the Pantasmas even bother coming to get him?

"You must rank highly in the Pantasmas," Juliet suddenly said, sounding a bit surprised.

Karter furrowed his eyebrows. "What makes you say that?" He had just been thinking the exact opposite.

"Why else would Alick and Sam themselves venture out to come get you? Those two have a price on their heads larger than half the kingdom's wealth."

Karter's eyebrows shot up. It was dangerous for Alick to leave the forest now that her name had been drawn. There were assassins crawling the kingdom trying to catch her when she least suspected it. But here she was, coming to get him, Karter, because he had been knocked out in a raid. Could he possibly be a bigger loser?

A knock on the door interrupted Karter's thoughts, and he struggled to sit up as Juliet opened the door to reveal two figures cloaked in black shrouds and surrounded by the reddish light of the setting sun.

If Karter hadn't known it was Sam and Alick at the door, he would have thought the devil himself had come to claim him.

"You two sure know how to make an entrance," Juliet commented as she hurried to get more teacups from her cupboards.

Karter watched as Alick smiled—the smile she used when she thought no one was watching. The one that meant: *they noticed I'm awesome!*

Then Alick spotted him, and concern engraved her features. Did he really look that bad?

"Where was he?" Alick asked, turning back to Juliet.

"In the valley. There was a lot of blood around. Whatever happened clearly involved more than just him and an attacker."

"There were two of them," Karter said, attempting to stand. About half way up, he got dizzy and fell over, causing Alick and Juliet to come rushing to his side. Sam stayed where she was, her eyebrows raised. *She probably thinks I'm a wimp,* Karter thought as Alick and Juliet helped him to a chair. But then he realized Sam wasn't looking at him; she was looking at Alick. *That's weird.*

"What in creation possessed you to run after them?" Alick asked.

Karter opened his mouth to answer, but shut it quickly when he noticed that Juliet was listening.

Alick followed his gaze and half nodded before turning to him, her questions burning in her eyes.

"I don't know," Karter finally said.

He saw Sam rolling her eyes and Juliet sigh, but Alick just nodded. She understood it was a story for private ears.

"Can he travel?" she asked Juliet, standing up again.

Juliet nodded. "He's much better than he was, and the tea I gave him should help."

Alick nodded again. She was doing that an awful lot.

"Juliet... do you know why the soldiers were camped on your farm?"

"I'm sorry, I don't. I assumed it was to catch you."

"Yes, that's what anyone would think..." Alick trailed off, looking deeply troubled. "No matter. They're gone now and will hopefully stay that way. Come on, Karter, it's best we left now." Karter nodded and got up, gathering his few things, careful to tuck the necklace away while no one was looking. He was glad Juliet hadn't said anything about it.

"Take care, Alick. Don't do anything reckless," Juliet cautioned.

Alick laughed dryly. "Reckless, whatever would give you that idea?"

CHAPTER 14

Honoring the dead had always been important in the Kingdom of Libre, though Fallon had been quick to abandon it. The Pantasmas, however, always followed tradition: it was a symbol of resistance that the Pantasmas more closely adhered to the rules of the lost city than to Fallon's rule.

So that night, once Alick and Sam had returned with Karter, the Pantasmas set out in the night to honor their fallen comrades, Bock and Eric.

The dark of the night seemed to close in on the Pantasmas as they walked through the forest, each holding a candle of remembrance. The leaves crunched beneath their feet and the wildlife teemed around them, but none of that mattered.

All that mattered was them, walking, cloaked in darkness and holding the orange, flickering candles that danced in the moonlight. The path they followed was thin and barely recognizable, and yet they never strayed from its borders as they walked in solemn silence.

Alick and Sam led the pack while Karter and Rydly brought up the rear, the path stretching on forever in the darkness. It wasn't until the moon was high in the sky that the Pantasmas reached their destination.

The tree loomed above everything else, its trunk so big that would take at least eight people to encircle it. The branches twisted and twined up into the sky, stretching across the clearing where the tree lived with elegance and grace. Leaves the size of a person's head clung to the tree, occasionally drifting down in the wind, landing gently on the ground in front of the Pantasmas.

Beyond the tree was a square plot of land fenced off with grey and rusting iron. Inside the plot, the shapes of graves could be made out in the moonlight, the graves of every Pantasma lost. Bock and Eric had been buried there earlier that day, and it was time to send their spirits to the heavens where they belonged.

The Pantasmas stopped only feet away from the tree and closed their eyes. A slight breeze blew through the clearing, making the leaves and branches sway and bringing to the Pantasmas a feeling of peace and relief though the candles flickered ominously.

In the front of the group, Alick opened her eyes and knelt on the ground, placing her candle in front of her. She raised her hands above her head, let the pads of her fingers touch and dropped her thumb, creating the image of a flame.

"In the darkness and the night, they were taken. Their bodies fell and their blood was spilt. Let their spirits now flow from our memories and our hearts into the Tree of Senciência." Alick stopped and took a deep breath, letting the smell of the grass and the trees fill her mind and bring peace to her heart before continuing. Losing a comrade was one of the most difficult things she had ever known in the world. "Though they are gone from this life, Eric and Bock have not left us forever. They are still here in our minds. In our memories. In our hearts. Their spirits will join those of our ancestors in the Tree of Senciência."

Behind her the other Pantasmas knelt, placed their candles on the ground, raised their hands into the flame symbol and said, "We honor those who have gone before and those who are still to come. We honor Bock and Eric. May their days above be filled with peace."

Silence overtook the Pantasmas as they sat there in remembrance. The candles flickered on the ground, the people hunched over in their cloaks, disguising their humanity. Alick breathed in the night air and began to sing the song of Libre.

Nature calls and nature sings
Nature brings us everything
the grass in the plain
the wind in the field
the sun on your face
and the rain on your skin

The power through the ages
is nature's sound
the power through the ages
is earth renowned
Hear it calling, hear its voice
Listen to its charming choice

Leaves turn yonder, watch them fly
through the misty mountain's cry
the thunder clapping
the lightning above
the earth as it calls

and nature when it sings

The power through the ages
is nature's sound
the power through the ages
is earth renowned
Hear it calling, hear its voice
Listen to its charming choice

Nature shows us all we need
All you have to do is see
the light in the forest
the stars in the night
the birds in the sky
and the beauty of all

The power through the ages
is nature's sound
the power through the ages
is earth renowned
Hear it calling, hear its voice
Listen to its charming choice

Hear the call and hear the voice
listen to nature's choice
it will give you all you need
all you have to do is believe

Alick finished and wiped a tear from her eye. As she began to sing it again, she stood up with her candle and began the long procession back to the Pantasma camp. The fallen had been honored; their spirits could rest in peace.

CHAPTER 15

Nothing the next day could distract Karter from thinking about the previous night. He'd been to funerals before, when his father lost soldiers, but this was the first one that had ever felt personal. It was the first one that felt real.

The other Pantasmas were walking around in a daze as well and the ones who had been the closest to the two fallen soldiers were zombies. Alick hadn't even emerged from her tent.

"How often does this happen?" Karter asked Rydly at one point.

"How often does what happen?"

"Pantasmas dying."

"Not as often as you might think. The most we ever lost was five in one year. That was hard," Rydly said with a sigh.

"That's going to change this year, isn't it?" Karter said somberly, remembering the coming battle.

"Karter, we'll be lucky if any of us survive this year."

The next several days passed in a similar manner. The Pantasmas went through the motions of the day, not really paying attention to anything, allowing their minds and hearts to heal.

Slowly, however, the Pantasmas began to act naturally again; the children played, laughter was plentiful, and activity against Fallon rose. Every night another squad returned with news of the annoyances they caused the King.

Karter watched it all from afar, feeling adrift in the sea of people. He still wasn't really one of them, though he tried, and he found their endless energy strange. What possessed these people to risk their lives day in and day out for a seemingly hopeless cause?

But Karter had made a decision to help them, and to prove himself he awoke every day at dawn with the warriors. The drills they did to keep their skills up were mostly beyond him, but Karter would try and try and after breakfast when the Pantasmas left to do their duties, he would keep practicing. While Rydly went about his chores, and

Alick and Sam worked with Peter on strategy, Karter was in the clearing reserved for swordplay, mauling dummies made of leaves. Sometimes Rydly or Alick would come spar with him, and sometimes he would spar with the warriors. Finally, when evening came, the entire camp was set up to spar—except for those too little to wield a weapon—and Karter would seek out the most skilled warriors to fight.

Almost three weeks later, his effort paid off.

"Karter, you're going with Robin's group today," Alick said when he sat by her at breakfast.

"What?"

"You heard me. You're headed out on duty today."

"But I still can't fight that well."

"It's a spy mission where Fallon's soldiers rarely pass, and you've been working really hard on your skills for almost a month. You should be fine."

This assessment was hardly comforting to Karter, but he joined the squad nevertheless, and they set off right as the sun reached its peak in the sky. He supposed if it was really dangerous they wouldn't let fourteen year old Robin lead it.

"All right, we're headed to the nearest wall junction to judge their progress. Our sources say

Fallon is planning to take the wall through the forest. We need to know where." Robin finished his speech and disappeared into the trees, leaving the rest of the squad and Karter to follow behind.

It always interested him how the Pantasmas said Fallon's name. Some uttered it with fear, others with a degree of reverence. But most, like Robin had, just spat out the name with the air of disposing of garbage.

Quickly, though, all of Karter's attention was focused on keeping up with the Pantasmas. He marveled at how fast they could move through the forest without making a sound. Karter, however, was conscious of his every thunderous footfall and every twig he stepped on. Each noise sounded like a gunshot despite the fact that the forest was far from quiet.

They ran for what seemed like hours, and Karter soon knew why. They were running to the edge of the forest.

The forest of the Pantasmas was huge, longer than the entire town and who knows how deep. It was the sort of place one only enters to get lost. Or to disappear. Karter had no problem accepting why the soldiers rarely ventured into the threatening wood, especially when it was inhabited by a bunch of deranged teenagers who rained havoc from the canopy.

And so Karter was shocked when the entire group came upon the farthest edge of the forest and even more shocked when he saw a host of men building a wall.

At a nod from Robin, the Pantasmas spread out along the tree line, hiding in the branches, to observe the work being done.

Karter, not knowing what else to do, began to count the men as they swarmed the wall. There must have been at least a hundred heaving bricks and mortar about. He remembered what Alick had said the when he'd woken in the Pantasma camp: *"If you were from here, you'd be dead, already a Pantasma, or working on Fallon's 'wall,'"* and Rydly's saying, *"His wall is a twenty foot high stone structure being built around the city by every-single able bodied man Fallon can find..."* Now Karter was looking at that exact wall.

He had a strange urge to run.

But at the same time, he knew that if this wall really did run all the way around the city... That could provide a huge advantage in battle. Possibly one that would change the odds. Higher ground always offered an advantage in battle. And it would be easier to block off supplies from the outside world when the city was contained by such a monolithic structure.

CHAPTER 16

*C*ould nothing go right? Two of her men were dead. Peter was clawing at the bit against her command. Layne had been captured by the city guards. Again. Sam and Rydly were fighting even more than usual, causing most of the camp to cower in their tents, and Karter was off with Robin on a reconnaissance of the wall that was threatening to cut through their woods. If the wall did come through the forest, that meant more soldiers in the woods. More soldiers, fewer Pantasmas. *Ugh.*

Alick sat in her tent staring dismally at the other side of the green-ish shelter. Some part of her wished for the time before Karter had shown up in their lives, before Heritor Day, when things had been simpler. The time when life had seemed like one big game and not a deadly war. The time when the Pantasmas rescued those in need and only stole what they needed to survive. But if they went back to that time, then Karter wouldn't be with them. Then Alick wouldn't have had a chance to reclaim what was hers by right.

Alick put her head in her hands and let out something between a sob, and a groan. She'd messed up. She shouldn't have accepted the chance to overthrow Fallon. Everyone had told her so, so why had she'd done it?

You didn't think about how much it was going to cost you. You made yourself believe that everything would somehow work itself out. You turned a blind eye when you should have stared ahead.

Sam came into the tent and Alick heard her sigh dramatically.

"Imagine, Karter has been back for ten minutes, and you haven't even noticed."

Alick's head shot up immediately on reflex. Embarrassed, she narrowed her eyes and glared at Sam. "That's not funny."

Sam laughed. "It was a little bit. And I was only half kidding."

"So Karter's really here?"

"No, but he will be soon. Robin sent a bird."

"Alick! Alick! Alick! Alick!" Piper came running into the tent screaming.

Alick and Sam both jumped.

"Piper, what is it?" Alick asked, worriedly.

"Peter killed the birdie!" Piper wailed before burying her head into Alick and continuing to sob.

Alick furrowed her eyebrows and looked up at Sam questioningly.

"Which bird?" she mouthed. The one from Robin?

Sam shrugged. *"How should I know?"* she mouthed back.

"It'll be okay, Piper," Alick murmured. "Peter will get in plenty of trouble."

"Promise?" Piper sniffled.

"Yes," Alick said solemnly. "Nobody should be so cruel."

"He was my very best birdie friend," Piper whispered.

Alick was horrified. She could not believe Peter killed a bird that clearly hung around camp regularly. They had a rule about that. She hugged the little girl closer. He was getting out of hand.

"I'm so sorry, Piper," she whispered.

Piper sniffed pathetically and curled herself into an even tighter ball. Within ten minutes she was sound asleep.

Alick looked down at the sleeping girl. "Don't you wish we could forget our troubles as easily?" she asked Sam.

Sam knelt and began to sharpen her knife. "We've been running from our troubles for ten years, Alick, don't you think it's about time they caught back up with us?"

Alick had no answer for that. "Sam, how are we ever going to attack Fallon?"

Sam shrugged. "Improvisation, probably."

"I'd like to know I was risking the Pantasmas lives on something a little more secure than that," Alick muttered.

Sam laughed. "Maybe Robin will have some good news."

"Good news from spying on Fallon? Unlikely," Alick sighed and began tidying the tent. Just something to keep her hands busy. "Who are we going to send into town to get Layne?"

Sam rolled her eyes. "Honestly, one of these days we should just leave that boy in the gallows."

"Sam!"

"I was kidding! Mostly, but seriously he has been caught by Fallon too many times, and one of these days we won't be *able* to rescue him."

Alick sighed. "You're right. But that doesn't help much."

Sam shrugged. "Send Robin when he gets back. Fallon's men won't recognize him, and he'll be able to glean plenty of information about the security of the city."

"He's so young, though."

"He's older than most, and directly under Peter."

"All right, but he better hurry up and return. I'm getting worried."

"Of course you are; this is the longest Karter has ever been out of your sight."

"Uh!" Alick's mouth dropped open in mock outrage, and she found the nearest pillow to chuck at Sam's head.

Sam simply picked the pillow up, sat on it, and continued sharpening her knife.

"You know it's not like that, Sam."

"Keep telling yourself that, Alick."

"I'm serious. I don't like Karter that way."

Sam looked up at Alick, a mischievous glint in her eye. "We'll see," she said.

Alick retort was lost as a horn sounded within the camp.

"Speaking of—"

Alick didn't wait for Sam to finish. She pushed out of the tent and bolted to the tree stump.

Scrambling to the top, Alick was able to see over the gathered Pantasmas to the edge of the clearing where Robin's party was just beginning to trickle in.

In Alick's peripheral vision she saw Sam exit Alick's tent and enter the command tent to prepare for the meeting to discuss Robin's find. Alick sighed and followed her, knowing that that was the proper place for her to be.

By the time Alick made her way to the tent, Rydly and Peter had arrived.

"Why is Riddle here?!" Sam asked.

"For the thousandth time, don't call me Riddle!" Rydly retorted.

Sam stuck her tongue out at him.

Alick sighed. Her friends were so immature at times it was unbelievable they were well into their teens. "Sam, Rydly's been here just as long as we have, and that gives him a right to plan against Fallon."

Sam made a face, but she didn't contradict.

A short while later, the tent flap opened up and Robin and Karter stepped in.

At the sight of Karter, Alick smiled widely, ignoring Sam's pointed stare.

"So, report?" Alick asked Robin.

"Not good. Fallon's going to cut through the forest, I'm sure of it, and his current trajectory brings him too close to the camp for comfort."

"Will we be inside or outside?"

"Outside, but barely."

"Strange," Alick murmured. "It's almost like he knows where we are."

"Or he's incredibly good at guessing," Peter muttered back. He was staring at the map on the central table. "Robin, where exactly is he now?"

Robin walked over, picked up a pen and extended Fallon's wall to mere centimeters from the forest line. Once he had finished, the group crowded around, anxious to see the wall's position.

"He'll just barely skim the top of our camp with that trajectory," Alick said.

Karter leaned over her shoulder to look, making Alick's heart skip several beats.

Alick shook her head to clear her thoughts. She couldn't afford to get any more attached to anyone in the Pantasmas. Not when they would all probably be dead soon. She had enough to worry about. "We'll have to move the camp," she said.

"Alick, that's a huge endeavor. We'd have to be able to hide our tracks, and that's difficult enough without having to drag all of our equipment." Peter put in.

"We don't really have a choice," Alick snapped. "We're not ready to take on Fallon. We have to move."

Her words had the same effect as someone sucking all the air out of the tent.

"How much time do we have?" Rydly asked finally.

Robin shook his head. "We probably have a week before they break the forest's edge. Then they'll only be a little more than a mile away."

"We'll move the Pantasmas two miles to the right, a mile below the great tree. We should be safe there for now." Alick's words rang out. *For now.* They all knew it was only a matter of time before they ran out of places to run.

CHAPTER 17

Moving camp sounded a lot easier than it was. And it didn't even sound easy. Karter had thought the entire Pantasma camp consisted of a few tents and peoples' possessions. The first few hours of packing quickly blew that idea out of Karter's mind and a few kingdoms over. First, there were the weapons amassed from raids. They were distributed among the Pantasmas until everyone was armed tooth and nail. The leftover weapons were shoved into clothing trunks and bundled carefully. Next there was the sheer number of people and food and clothing. It took nearly three days before the entire camp was contained in packages for moving.

"How on earth can a band of thieves have so much stuff?!" Karter exclaimed to Rydly as they hefted another trunk onto the growing pile.

"Um... the thieves part?" Rydly answered.

Karter opened and closed his mouth a few times like a guppy. He hadn't thought that question through very well.

"Karter!" Alick called, causing said boy to trip over a root as he looked over his shoulder toward her.

"Yeah, Alick," Karter gasped, pinching himself to keep from screaming. With his luck, his toe was probably broken. Rydly was no help, he was too busy trying not to laugh.

"How many of these trunks do you think you can carry at once?" She asked, her eyebrows furrowing in an adorable look of concern.

"Um, a third of one," Karter replied, still mentally cursing his toe.

Alick laughed and shook her head. "I was serious. We're moving them tomorrow, so you'd better get some rest." Alick began to walk off again. At the last minute, she turned around and said, "Rydly, make sure he sticks his foot in the river for a while. We can't have a limping soldier."

Karter cursed under his breath; she *had* seen him trip. "Does she think I was kidding about the heaviness of the trunks?" he asked Rydly as he hobbled toward the river.

Rydly nodded, "Yes, she does. And in case you're wondering—tripping over a root? Smooth."

Karter glared at him. "You are no help."

"Dude, if you want Alick to like you, it doesn't help if you're incapacitated because you ran into a tree."

"Oh, ha ha. It's not as easy as it sounds to avoid them."

"And yet you have managed to completely avoid the fact that I just accused you of liking Alick."

"Accused me? You make it sound like it's illegal."

"So you *do* like her."

"I never said that," Karter argued. By now they had reached the river, though river may have been a bit of a misnomer. A more appropriate name for the body of water would be rushing stream of doom. At least that's how Karter felt after he slipped on the wet rocks, fell in, and got pushed downstream several feet before managing to fight the current.

"The river gods seem to disagree with you," Rydly said, still laughing at the now wet and limping Karter.

"River gods, that's a good one," Karter muttered. He sat down on the bank and dipped his injured foot into the cold waters, shivering. "So why are you suddenly interested in how I view Alick?"

"I'm not really. I just find it amusing that you seem ten times less coordinated when she's around."

Karter frowned. "Rydly, I just fell in a river. Again. Don't you think it's possible I'm just a klutz?"

"Karter, klutzes don't take to sword fighting like they were born to it."

Karter sighed. It was true, he was improving miraculously quickly in his sword fighting lessons. But really, when Sam and or Alick was threatening to impale you and you practiced every waking minute, you learned quickly.

"Karter, I just want the two of you to be happy. That's not a common emotion in times like these."

"And friends can't be happy?"

Rydly shrugged. "I guess," he said.

Karter narrowed his eyes. He knew Rydly still thought he liked Alick. He just hoped it wouldn't come back to haunt him.

"Do you think I can walk on it yet?" he asked, changing the subject.

Rydly bent forward to look at Karter's foot, tinted blue under the water.

"Hard to tell, can you move it?"

Karter wiggled his toes and gasped when it hurt. "Seriously!" he vented as soon as he got his breath back. "All I did was trip over a root! This is ridiculous."

Rydly smirked. "That'll teach you."

"Teach me what?"

"To act flustered around girls."

Karter narrowed his eyes. "You'll pay for that when I can walk again."

"Which better be quick if you want to show Alick your strength tomorrow," Rydly quipped before quickly scooting out of Karter's reach.

"You'd better shut it or I'll tell Sam you like her."

"Wait... what? I do *not* like Sam!" Rydly stood on his feet, clearly outraged.

"Dude, calm down, it was a joke." Karter took his foot out of the water and gently wiggled his toes, smiling when it didn't hurt as much. His toes were numb from the ridiculously cold river, though, so maybe he just couldn't feel the pain. "But with a reaction like that..." Karter implied, trailing off.

"You drop it, I'll drop it," Rydly said.

"Fair enough." Karter put his shoe back on, and together they walked back to camp. Karter would have to find a change of clothes if he didn't want to spend the rest of the night dripping. Stupid river.

CHAPTER 18

Getting the camp moved was going smoothly, relatively speaking, but Alick still could not relax. Scouts reported that the wall was moving ever closer, and the pace was picking up. The section of wall being worked on was close enough to town that replacements for worn out men were in quick supply, which meant construction was practically constant.

"Good news," Peter said, coming into the command tent where Alick sat alone, staring at the map.

"Does that even exist anymore?" Alick murmured.

"What?" Peter asked, leaning closer. Alick rolled her eyes. Peter didn't understand.

"Nothing, what's the news?" Alick said audibly.

"The camp's packed and ready. All that's left is this tent."

"The rest has been packed and moved?"

"Well... it's been packed."

Alick nodded. "Have everyone pitch in with moving. I want the camp transferred by nightfall. Fallon's drawing too close too soon."

Peter nodded, practically bowing, and ducked back out of the tent.

Alick sat back down and put her head in her hands. The sooner she could get her people moved, the better. She didn't want to lose anyone else. One of the scouts had been caught just that morning and been beaten up pretty bad. He'd survived, but barely, and it would be touch and go for a few days to see if he really pulled out of it.

"Um... should I come back later?" It was Karter, of course; the Pantasmas didn't really have manners.

Alick lifted her head back up. "You're fine. What's wrong?"

"The trunks are heavy. The children can't lift them and neither can most of the soldiers."

"Ugh. All right. Have Robin call back everyone. Leave only the scouts between us and the wall." Alick frowned. She despised leaving the camp unprotected, but they needed to move.

Karter nodded, also practically bowing. Why did people do that? Was she being that authoritative? She was in charge, but she wasn't the Queen. Yet.

"Alick?"

"What?!"

"No need to snap, I simply came to help you pack up the tent."

"Sorry, Sam," Alick sighed.

"It's fine. You've been bothered quite a bit today." Sam replied with a mischievous glint in her eye.

Alick just rolled her eyes and began rolling up the maps on the table.

"Why on earth do we have so many maps?" Sam exclaimed as she lifted up the lid of the one trunk in the room.

"What else are we to look at when we are unwelcome in the world?"

"I was being serious."

"And how do you know I wasn't?"

Sam shrugged and walked around the tent, taking down more maps and placing them on the table for Alick to roll. They continued in this way for quite a while; outside, the sliding and shifting of heavy trunks and the *oofs* of those carrying them could be heard.

"Sam, do you think I can really lead these people?"

"No one else can, Alick. You're their Queen."

"That was never a title I wanted."

"Maybe you should have thought of that before agreeing to fight Fallon for the crown."

"I should never have done that, Sam."

Sam looked up at her and smiled sadly. "There's no going back. This was meant to happen, and it was meant to happen to you."

"How can I ask the Pantasmas to fight alongside me? It's a suicide mission."

"They'll follow you anywhere."

"How many times will you have to convince me to keep going?"

Sam smiled, and she and Alick laughed. It was not a joyful laugh, rather the laugh one shares with a friend when one realizes that they know you more about you than you do.

"I imagine we will lose faith many times before the end, Alick. As long as we don't all lose faith at once."

Alick smiled wide and laughed to herself.

"What?" Sam demanded.

"Once again, Sam, you have let your rebel exterior drop to show the wisdom beneath the teeth."

"Oh, ha ha. Good cop, bad cop has kept this group in line for years," Sam defended.

"I fear that as the noose tightens, the roles are switching."

"Your strength does not lie in force, Alick. Not to worry."

By this time, they had finished rolling the maps and placed them neatly in the trunk.

"This thing is heavy," Sam complained, hefting the trunk.

"What did you expect?" Alick groaned, straining under the weight.

They were lucky to make it outside before they dropped the trunk.

"I told you those things were heavy," Karter called from where he and Rydly were trying to lift a much larger trunk than the one Alick and Sam had just dropped.

"I need a break," Alick said as she surveyed the organized chaos that was the moving effort. She felt weary to the bone and moving the trunk hadn't helped, though she felt like a wimp for admitting it. She hadn't slept more than two hours since they'd decided to move the camp, though, so that was probably part of it.

"Go to the tree, Alick. I'll take care of it."

"I can't do that, Sam, I'm needed here."

"It'll be fine. You've been working to help move us nonstop. You've barely even slept, and you've not eaten properly in days."

"Fine. I'll meet you at the new encampment at sunset." Alick turned and entered the woods, careful to make sure no Pantasmas saw her disappear. A break was hardly a break if someone could follow you.

CHAPTER 19

Only Karter saw Alick slip away into the forest, and he was wise enough not to say anything. Out of habit, he slid his hand into his tunic and felt the pendant that he still had hidden there. He should show it to Alick, but if Fallon wanted it bad enough to send an entire host of soldiers to retrieve it, the fact that Karter had it needed to be kept as secret as possible. In a band of kids, the only way to do that was to show Alick and *only* Alick. Something that was significantly easier said than done. Especially when she was busy trying to organize patrols around the newly forming wall.

Karter was quickly and unexpectedly jerked out of his reverie when a trunk landed solidly on his foot.

"Ow!" Karter yelped, jumping backwards and tripping over the same root he had fallen over earlier talking to Alick.

"Smooth, Karter," Peter called, laughing. "Next time stop daydreaming!"

Karter narrowed his eyes as Rydly helped him stand up again. He was tired of being laughed at all the time.

"Why is he so snappy?" Karter grumbled, rubbing his foot.

"He takes his position as third in command very seriously, and he dislikes Sam with a passion. I think his private hope is that someday he can replace her as Alick's right hand."

"Yeah, well, good luck with that. I still don't understand why you're not third in command."

"Depends on the context. I am not one to lead a battalion."

"I know what you mean. Neither am I."

"You're wrong."

"What?"

"I said, you're wrong. Karter, everyone here knows that you are exactly the person who should lead a battalion."

"You're joking, only jerks lead battalions, plus, I still can't spar any of the Pantasmas and win."

"All of that may be true, but you have a characteristic that most of us lack."

"And what is that characteristic that apparently everyone but me can see?" Karter asked testily.

"Courage. Defiance. Honor." Rydly began listing the traits off on his fingers.

Karter blinked and shook his head. "What exactly have I done to convince you people I have any of those characteristics? Plus you guys have them too."

"Not the same way. Not the way you do."

"Well how do I have them?" Karter pried, still annoyed because his foot hurt.

"Well, you're not from here."

"Yeah."

"And you stayed."

"So?"

"So, any person in this city with a sane mind would jump at a chance to leave and never look back. Especially if they were mixed up in all this Fallon business."

"I stayed because I'm your prisoner."

"Karter, you could have asked to be let go at any time. We would have sworn you to secrecy and shown you back to town where you could have found a way out of town again. Don't tell me you didn't know that."

Karter looked down at his feet. He had known that. These thieves were not kidnappers. But did staying really make Karter courageous? Stupid, maybe. Defiant? Whom had he ever defied in his life? Karter couldn't see honorable either, but he supposed he wasn't dishonorable.

"I still don't think you're right," he told Rydly as they walked back to camp to get another trunk.

"I am, though. I hear all the gossip that flows through the Pantasmas."

"And what exactly does this gossip say about me?" Karter asked curiously, ducking under a low tree branch.

"Let's just say you have quite the fan club."

Karter looked at Rydly incredulously, but their arrival at camp postponed any further questioning when they saw the chaos that had erupted. It seemed to do that a lot.

"What is going on?" Rydly gasped. The camp was even more aflutter with activity, if that was possible. Trunks were being lifted away by everybody, sometimes requiring ten children to a trunk just to get it off the ground. Others were running about disguising the tracks made by the camp, hiding the fact that the Pantasmas were ever there.

Sam ran by, wild-eyed.

"Sam," Rydly called. "What's happening?"

Sam jogged back, never entirely ceasing to move as she told them. "The soldiers have marched ahead. They'll be here within the hour. We have to get everything moved NOW."

Rydly's jaw dropped and he quickly moved off to help, but Karter grabbed Sam's arm, the desperateness of the situation the only reason why he wasn't flipped over her shoulder for doing so.

"What about Alick?"

"What about her?"

"She won't know," Karter said.

Sam's eyes lit up with recognition and she bit her lip.

"Karter, do you think you can find the big tree again?"

"The one where we had the funerals?"

"Yes, that one."

"I don't know; I suppose so."

"Run, run there. That's where Alick went, I'm sure of it. Tell her what's happening, and don't let her leave until sunset. There's no way we'll be able to completely obscure our tracks in this clearing, though we might manage between the clearing and our new camp. Either way, these woods will be crawling with soldiers and she *cannot be caught.*"

Karter nodded. "Got it, I won't let you down."

"It's her you can't let down, Karter."

Karter nodded again, and then he turned around and took off into the forest, praying he could find his way and that they could get moved ahead of the advancing soldiers.

CHAPTER 20

utterflies flittered through the branches, and the green leaves fluttered in the breeze. The clear blue sky, just barely visible from Alick's perch in the Great Tree, beckoned her to fly, while below the large branches, the graves of the fallen Pantasmas and Alick's parents were just barely visible through the thick foliage. It was a peaceful spot, but it contained more sad memories than any other place Alick knew besides the castle.

Alick was still plagued by the nightmares of Fallon's slaughter. All the nobles, twenty or thirty at most, had been in the castle, gathered for the biggest ball of the year, the King's birthday. The celebrations had been due to begin the next morning when even the commoners would stream into the castle ballroom for the most fantastic night of the season.

Little did anyone know they would never get the chance.

Alick remembered it all: the cold, menacing eyes of Fallon watching her throughout dinner, it was the first time she had met Kana's newest suitor. Alick's parents had sent her to bed soon after desert, their kind eyes smiling as she hugged them goodnight. It would be the last time she ever saw them.

"Alick?"

Karter's voice, coming from below, jerked Alick out of her dark thoughts as a tear rolled down one cheek. Why was he here?

"Alick?!"

Something was wrong. Why did Karter sound so panicked?

"Up here," Alick called, looking down and catching Karter's eye.

"Thank goodness, Alick." Karter sighed. He scrambled up into the tree and sat opposite her, using the trunk of the tree as a backrest just as Alick used the strange shape of the branch.

"Karter, what's wrong?" Why was he settling in if he sounded so panicked? She felt a familiar anxiety bubbling up inside, fearing the worst.

"The guards on the wall began to scout ahead, so we had to speed up the moving of the camp. It should be done now, I think. When I left, they only had an hour until the men arrived. Sam sent me to make sure you don't get caught. We're not to leave for the new location until nightfall."

Alick let out the breath she had been holding. Not life or death. Not yet. She prayed with all her soul that they had gotten everything moved. Sam was no idiot, though; she would have abandoned the stuff and just moved the people if need be.

"I would have been fine," Alick muttered, though truthfully part of her was glad that Karter had come. It did her no good to wallow in the tragedies of the past. She did like the tranquility of the spot, though.

"We can't very well take that chance, though, can we?" Karter asked, attempting to joke.

Alick smiled wryly. "I guess not."

And for the next hour or so, they just sat there, enjoying the silence of the clearing, watching the butterflies and the clouds as they blew across the sky, barely visible between all the foliage. The quiet environment, such a contrast from the bustling camp, was peaceful in a way that felt almost magic.

Alick found her thoughts drifting to Karter to keep her mind off of her parents and their fate. She watched as he furrowed his brow. There was a crease between his eyebrows. It was cute. A breeze came through and ruffled his hair, throwing his features into stark contrast, and Alick was once again reminded of his regal nature, of the idea that there was more to Karter than he shared.

"Karter, what's your name?" she asked, almost without meaning too.

"What?" Karter looked at her and his expression of sheer confusion was enough to send Alick into a fit of giggles. It felt so good to laugh again. It was such a place of beauty that it felt wrong to be sad.

"What's your full name, Karter?" Alick rephrased.

"Why do you want to know?" Karter asked. He was different now; his eyes were guarded.

Alick cocked her head to one side and thought before answering. Finally she said, "You are a mystery, Karter. I'm just curious, that's all." She didn't understand his reaction. He was hiding something; that much was obvious. She leaned her head back against the tree trunk, wondering if it had been a mistake to trust Karter so implicitly. What if he was a spy for Fallon? His spirit wasn't broken, though... Still, secrets had a cost. They were always more dangerous than they seemed.

After what seemed like an eternity of silence, in which Alick's head spun through every scenario that could possibly exist, Karter finally spoke again.

"Like you, Alick, I come from a noble family, but from a kingdom where twins aren't allowed to exist in any family that could potentially be crowned king."

Alick squinted her eyes in thought. "So wait... someone could be twentieth in line for the throne and still not be able to have twins?"

Karter nodded. Of all the scenarios Alick had considered, this had not been one of them.

"The idea is to keep peace in throne succession. With twins there can always be disputes over who was actually born first."

Alick shook her head in confusion. "Okay... so you're the younger twin?"

Karter nodded, looking uneasy. "I was actually the older of the two of us, but I was a weak child. Everyone thought Balthazar was older, so I was the one that was banished."

Alick had no idea how to respond to such a story. It was so sad, almost worse than hers. Alick couldn't imagine having parents that chose your sibling over you because of physical strength. Knowing you were least loved... It was horrible.

Alick looked up and noticed Karter was clutching one of his shirt pockets.

Momentarily diverted from Karter's story, Alick sat up straighter. "What's that?"

Karter blinked, looking unsure, and then he pulled out the last thing Alick thought would ever end up in Karter possession.

"Where did you get that?" Alick asked, awe in her voice. She hadn't seen the necklace since she was a little girl in the palace. It had been one of her most prized possessions. Alick reached out and gingerly took the trinket from Karter's hand, reveling in the sharp edges of the symbol she had known since birth.

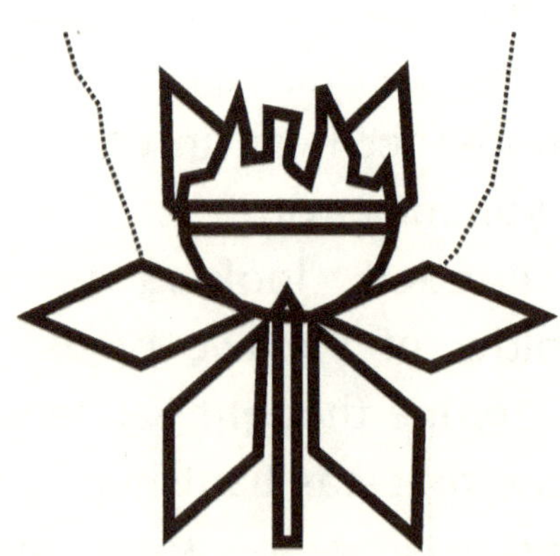

To see it again it such a place of memory was almost too good to be true. It was like she'd been dropped back into her own time stream, a little girl with an infinite realm of possibilities laid out before her.

"It's my crista real," Alick whispered, still awestruck.

"What's a crista real?" Karter asked.

Alick's head snapped up. She had almost forgotten Karter was there. She'd almost told him her own secret.

"Its um... a family crest," Alick stammered. It was mostly the truth.

"What does it mean?" Karter asked, sounding intrigued. Alick supposed there was no harm in answering that. Especially if he hadn't already recognized it. Anyone else in the Pantasmas would have immediately known what it was and who it belonged to. She would have been busted.

"Well," Alick pointed to the six diamonds. "These are the six morals my family lives by: unity, loyalty, kindness, strength, bravery, and honor. And the torch is our symbol, chosen by my distant ancestors to denote their trade."

"What was the trade?"

"They were *chama portadores.* Flame bringers."

"What does that mean?"

Alick smiled, remembering when she asked her mother the exact same question.

"They brought the flame that conquered these lands. But they did not conquer by force; they were given the land because the people were in such awe of the flames that they brought."

"But where did they get the flames, mommy?"

"From the most regal beast of them all, the dragon. Legend has it, our ancestors had a special relationship with the dragons and helped hide them away where they would be safe from the world in exchange for their fire. And it was with the dragon's fire that they built their city and named it Libre in honor of the free spirits of the dragons."

As the memory faded away, Alick remembered a very important piece of information. *The dragons were still around.* Alick had the same blood as her ancestors, and more importantly, she had the very trinket that had been passed down generation after generation. The most important artifact in the world. One she could use.

The talisman had been forged by her ancestor from dragon claw in their home mountains by dragon fire. It was a symbol of the friendship that had existed.

Looking up at Karter, Alick had a dangerous and potentially fatal idea. But first she had to be sure. She had to know positively that she was doing the right thing. It would be foolish to go off on a potentially suicide mission without absolute proof it could work.

"Karter, where did you get this?"

Karter gave her a look and Alick realized she had never answered his question. Too late for that now. Whoops.

"I took it from the knights I chased the night of the raid. I don't think they realized I took it, or the one that got away wouldn't have left me alive. It seemed too important to show you when we weren't alone."

Alick let that information sink in. If what Karter said was true, then Alick finally knew why Fallon had put his men in Juliet's fields. He had discovered the path she'd taken when she'd escaped and he had gone to look for it, assuming she'd dropped it. That could only mean two things. Either Fallon had had the same stupid, dangerous, potentially fatal idea that she had had, or he knew that she would try it. Either way, it proved to Alick that this was her genuine crista real. It would work.

With that knowledge, Alick made her decision.

"Karter?"

"Yes?"

"I'm going to go on a trip very far from here, and I may not come back." She wasn't entirely sure why she told him. It just seemed like the natural thing to do. Plus, he would probably take it a lot better than Sam and Rydly. Though he was more than likely going to think her mentally addled after this entire exchange.

Karter was silent for a while, and then slowly, he answered.

"Then I'm coming with you."

Alick was so taken aback by the response, it took her a minute to process it. When she finally did, she smiled wide and laughed.

"You don't even know where we're going yet."

"Doesn't matter. It has something to do with that trinket, and I'm not going to let you do it alone. Two have a better chance than one."

Alick couldn't doubt the truth of that. It was why she and Sam were so close. They always stood a better chance in battle together than apart.

The setting sun chose that moment to pass directly perpendicular to Alick and Karter, shining the last light of the day on the tree and bathing it in an ethereal golden light for just a moment before disappearing behind the horizon, leaving the clouds lit up in splendid colors.

For a moment, Alick stared into the clouds, marveling at time. It was a funny thing; when you wanted it to slow down, all it ever seemed to do was go faster and faster.

"Come on," she said with a sigh. "It's getting dark, and Sam and Rydly will send out a search party if we don't come back soon."

"Are they going to come with us too? On our journey?"

"No, someone has to stay and watch the camp." Alick's insides twisted slightly as she said that. Truthfully, Peter could probably watch the camp himself. But she didn't trust him, not with that much responsibility. Peter was too warlike, too reckless. He'd probably march on Fallon the minute she left. Sam would be much better. Alick dropped from the tree and began to walk. She couldn't leave Sam alone though. Too much bad cop, not enough good cop would turn the Pantasmas against her. Rydly could be good cop. But could the two of them work together?

"Alick?"

"Yeah, Karter?" They were almost to the edge of the clearing, and they would have to sneak through the underbrush once they hit the woods. What did he want to ask her now? Was he reconsidering coming with her? She wouldn't blame him.

"Where are we going to go?"

Alick smiled in spite of herself. She knew she was going to sound crazy, and she half expected Karter to rescind his offer of companionship. She herself was beginning to wonder if she should have made this decision while half-mad from sleep deprivation.

"We're going to find the dragons, Karter." Alick said, holding her head high, daring him to challenge her. "We're going to find them, and then we're going to bring them back, and we're going to beat Fallon once and for all."

CHAPTER 21

Zigzagging back through the trees, the darkness of night closing in around them, Karter and Alick were both silent; thinking about the task they had unwisely chosen to take. Alick's words kept reverberating around inside Karter's head. *"We're going to find the dragons."* She was crazy. She had to be. There were no dragons; they were mythical creatures of storybooks and legends meant to frighten children into behaving.

They reached a clearing, and, looking up, Karter saw a cloud cross the moon, a cloud that, just for a minute, looked like a dragon. Karter shook his head. *There are no such things as dragons*, he told himself repeatedly. And yet he made no move to tell Alick, no move to suggest that he didn't think that what they were going to do was possible.

It was the look on Alick's face that stopped him. For the first time since her name had been called out, she looked hopeful.

She thought that dragons existed with a fervor that made Karter sure she had intel that he didn't. Or she'd finally gone crazy. Either scenario was possible. He was really banking on the first one though.

Not for the first time, Karter wondered just who her parents had been. That family crest of hers was old. Karter remembered seeing it in a history book from his youth. If only he could remember the words that had accompanied it, or what trade "flame bringers" practiced.

Why had he even volunteered to go with her? Before he knew where they were going? He told himself it was his sense of camaraderie. But in his heart, Karter knew differently. He wanted to go with Alick because he was curious.

He wanted to know what she had been thinking about, what she had remembered when she had stared off into the foliage for so long. The trinket was a part of her past, and it held information that she had forgotten, information that Karter deeply wanted to know.

Karter was so lost in his thoughts that he didn't notice that Alick had stopped until he ran into her.

She shot him a look that was both annoyed and amused.

"Sorry," he whispered. "Why did we stop?"

"This is a highly travelled path by Fallon's men. We should be cautious." Alick whispered back. "And stealthy," she added, her voice getting quieter with each word as she sank to the ground and began to creep into the bushes that lined the road. Karter furrowed his eyebrows but followed her, unsure of what was going on. He had just crawled into the bushes when he heard the noise. Hoofbeats, coming closer, fast.

"Alick!" Karter hissed, searching the underbrush carefully for his friend. "Where are you?" He was getting frantic now. The hoofbeats were almost upon them. He was visible from above, yet he was too large to disappear like Alick had.

Karter whipped around; he could see the horse now, its rider cloaked and hidden, headed right for them. He felt a yank on his ankle and then there was darkness. Darkness and the smell of dank earth.

"What's going on?" Karter said, or tried to say. Alick's hand was over his mouth. Overhead, the hoofbeats slowed and Karter heard the rider dismount. Beside him, Alick tensed, and Karter caught the glint of a dagger. He swallowed, loudly, earning a glare from Alick.

Karter practically held his breath until the footsteps retreated and the hoofbeats returned, headed away from them. Then they both breathed.

"That was close," Alick whispered. She looked whiter then usual, but that might have been because they were underground...

"Where are we, Alick?"

"A tunnel that leads to the camp."

"The new camp isn't underground."

"No, but now that we're leaving I'm wondering if it should be."

Beyond that, conversation halted; there was no light in the tunnel, and Karter was spending all his energy and focus trying to find his way through without running into Alick again. He felt rather useless all of a sudden, having almost been caught, and was admiring how Alick and her band of thieves had managed to stay alive and elusive all these years.

After a while, however, Karter had to say something. "How long is this tunnel?" he asked, annoyed that he sounded out of breath.

"A good couple of miles. It's not the most direct route we could take, but it's a whole lot safer."

Karter felt his gut clench. He knew in his heart that they were taking this tunnel because of him. He was not the stealthiest person, and one day, living like this, it was going to come back and bite him. He could only imagine the teams of guards stalking the forest floor above, looking for their targets that were so incredibly elusive.

It wasn't until Karter thought he would never breathe fresh air again that Alick finally led him up and out of the tunnel into a dark clearing.

How does no one find the hole? Karter wondered just as Alick moved a bush back into place over the opening. Karter felt stupid. He hadn't even realized that she had moved the bush to get out of the tunnel.

Alick brushed the dirt off her pants and stood up, offering Karter her hand.

"It will be dark under the trees, and I wouldn't want you to get lost," Alick said.

Karter furrowed his brow but took Alick's hand as she led him through the trees and bushes to the camp. The leaves clung to their clothes, and the damp dirt sank through their pants on the knees as they stayed low in the brush. They couldn't hear any soldiers, and they weren't a quiet bunch, but it never hurt to be careful.

There was no bonfire tonight. No warm cauldron of soup to soothe the Pantasmas. Instead they were all huddled around the cool and as of yet unused fire pit, whispering and murmuring amongst themselves.

"We're back," Alick said, somewhat unnecessarily, as all the heads turned and started at Karter and Alick.

Sam detached herself from the crowd and flung her arms around Alick, looking relieved. Karter couldn't hear what Sam said, but he would bet money that Sam was berating Alick for making the Pantasmas worry. Just wait until they found out their plan with the dragons. Sam might explode. That would be extremely entertaining to watch, especially if Rydly thought it was a good idea.

Karter was jerked back to reality by a sharp pain on his bicep.

"What was that for?" Karter yelped; Sam had hit him.

"For taking so long!"

"You told me to wait until sunset to let her leave the clearing," Karter muttered.

"Yes, well, you could have been faster about it. The sun set nearly an hour ago."

"It was slow going, Sam." Alick jumped in, "The woods are still being patrolled by Fallon's men."

"At this rate, I'm not sure they'll ever stop." Peter came up, eager to be a part of the discussion. Karter smiled as he watched Alick flinch slightly at the added audience.

"Have any of you eaten?" Alick quickly changed the subject.

Sam shook her head. "Didn't want to start the fire."

To Karter's surprise, Alick looked relieved.

"Peter, can you go see if you can find some bread or something for the children? You know how they are when their stomachs are empty."

Karter smirked as Peter moved off with a stormy look in his eyes. He never seemed to learn —the more he tried to gain power, the more Alick shunted him. If he just contented himself with where he was in the chain of command, remembered that he was in charge of military not domestic activities, she wouldn't downgrade him so much.

"Karter, find Rydly and bring him to the command tent." Alick smiled slightly, but Karter could see she was exhausted.

"Why do you continue to include Rydly in important discussions, like the one you obviously have in mind? Before this debacle with being "chosen" and all, he was never a part of the command circle!" Sam suddenly ranted.

Alick turned to her friend, surprised. "Sam, this is no longer about military strength or prowess. Combatting Fallon is no longer our first priority. We have to stay hidden. We've been given a chance of a lifetime, but we can only succeed if we all stay alive until we're absolutely ready." Alick paused; Sam was rolling her eyes.

She knew she was repeating herself, but Alick continued anyway. "If Fallon succeeds in picking us all off one by one, there won't be any Pantasmas to rise up and take the throne. There is only one quality in my command circle that can ensure that."

"What quality?" Karter butted in. Alick started; she hadn't realized he was still there.

Alick raised an eyebrow at him.

"I'm going to get Rydly," Karter said defensively, starting to back away. "But what quality?"

"Trust," Alick said. As Karter backed away, Sam added, "And you trust Karter and Rydly more than you trust Peter."

"Why wouldn't I, Sam?"

"I understand trusting Rydly, but we've known Karter for scarcely anytime at all. Why do you trust him so?"

Alick shrugged. She honestly had no clue, but she couldn't tell Sam that; she'd never live it down. "He understands what's going on. He gets it."

"Peter does, too."

"No, Peter is too pugnacious. He'd just as soon engage every man in the forest to a personal duel."

"You have a point there," Sam grudgingly admitted.

"What do you have against Karter anyway?"

"I just don't want to see you hurt, Alick. That's happened plenty enough."

CHAPTER 22

Papers covered everything in the command tent. Maps, battle plans, lists... Anything helpful Alick or one of her people had ever written down in the struggle against Fallon. Before Heritor Day, the mess had been contained to the large table that took up most of the tent. But now the paper proliferated the tent so fully, it was difficult to find places to walk.

"So, what's up?" Sam asked once she and Alick were in the privacy of the tent. "You're hiding something; I can tell."

"I have a plan."

"Very good. Plans are golden."

"You're not going to like it."

"I never do."

"It's dangerous, risky, and *highly* unlikely to work."

"Aren't they all? Now tell me, because boy one and boy two will be back soon."

"Sam, they have names," Alick replied as she pulled out the necklace she'd taken from Karter in the tree. "Do you recognize this?" she asked.

Sam shook her head. "Just the symbol in the middle. It's arcane and not often used."

"And what does it mean?"

Sam bit her lip. "Dragon."

Alick smiled grimly. "This is my Crista Real, Sam."

Sam's eyes widened. "No way. Where'd you find it? I thought Fallon would have destroyed anything with the noble family crests. And I know they have names, I just don't use them."

"This particular trinket is too important to be destroyed, and Fallon knew it. I wonder how he found it... I lost it that night while running from him. To think, the expedition on Juliet's farm was probably all to find this. He was never after us at all..." Alick trailed off, looking at the trinket in wonder. "And its dehumanizing not to use their names. Lord knows we have enough of that in this kingdom."

"Fine, I'll be respectful, but will you *please* start from the beginning? I'm not following you at all," Sam said as she sank into the nearest chair.

"When Rydly gets here—"

Alick cut off as Karter and Rydly ducked into the tent.

"Okay, then I guess I'll start," Alick said. "First, I... no that's not important." Alick began shifting from foot to foot, trying to decide how best to express herself. She was ever aware of her friends' gazes. She knew they would despise this plan and the anxiety that caused was turning her stomach in knots. She was starting to doubt herself, and that was never a good sign.

"Okay. This is my family crest." She showed Rydly the necklace as Karter and Sam nodded. "When I was running from Fallon on the night he ransacked the palace, I dropped it. I didn't remember when or where, and it quickly faded from my mind.

"Somehow... somehow Fallon found it; he knew its power, and either wanted to use it for himself or just wanted to make sure I couldn't use it—"

"How did you find it?" Rydly asked.

"I found it," Karter interrupted. "That man I chased down the night of the raid was attempting to smuggle it to safety. I took it from him without him realizing."

"How could you possibly have taken that without him realizing?" Sam asked.

Karter shrugged, setting off a loud debate primarily featuring Sam and Rydly as Karter sat uncomfortably in the middle.

"Guys!" Alick regained order. "Doesn't matter."

"You still haven't told us what this thing does that makes it so important," Sam grumbled, crossing her arms.

"Yeah, there's a reason for that..."

"Like what?" Sam insisted, sitting back up.

"You're going to think I'm crazy, Sam." Alick said, desperation lacing her voice and weariness enveloping her with every breath.

"Alick, we're here because we're your friends. You can tell us," Rydly cut in kindly.

Alick bit her lip and sighed. "It's supposed to show the dragons that my family is friends with them. Supposedly, it allows us to gain their trust and they'll help us when we're in need," she said really quickly, her eyes shut.

Alick opened one eye and was met with the blank stares of Sam and Rydly; Karter just looked amused, though she wasn't sure why.

Sam opened and closed her mouth, seemingly grasping for words.

"I know it sounds crazy, but... I don't know, why would Fallon care so much about it if the legends weren't true?"

"Do we know that Fallon really cared for it? Maybe that guard was just a coward and happened to have found your trinket?" Rydly put in.

"I suppose. But it's worth a shot, isn't it?" Alick was desperate. She needed this to work. They were too few against too many. More importantly, she needed her two closest friends to believe it, to believe her.

"Alick, you can't possibly think you'll find the dragons. Even if there were any to be controlled, where would we even begin to look?" Alick suppressed a groan; she hated it when Sam used logic against her.

Alick sat down in her chair and stared at the torches lining the tent, their flames flickering, searching for substance while shadows danced around. "I don't know, Sam," she sighed. As if to spite her, the shadows began to look more and more like dragons.

"The northern mountain range," Karter said.

Alick turned to him. "What?"

Karter looked uneasy. "In my kingdom, we always heard stories of the impassable mountain range; those that tried to cross it were never seen again. Traders who live by the foothills swear there are monsters on the heights that catch their prey with fire hot enough to melt stone."

"Dragons," Alick whispered, almost to herself.

Karter nodded. "Most likely."

"How do we find the mountains from here?"

"On most maps I've seen, the mountain range spans nearly the whole continent. If we just head north, we're bound to find it."

"Finding the beasts within is bound to be harder, though, especially given they don't exist," Sam put in. "Plus, there's a reason most countries are walled and travelers never stray from the road. Strange creatures do roam the land."

"But this country was never walled," Karter pointed out, sounding confused.

"This country was founded by the Flame Bringers; no other creatures would come near a dragon den. The dragons stayed long enough that the creatures found other places to live, and they still avoid this place." Sam recited the bedtime story all little children of Libre had learned—there was no reason to fear that trolls would steal socks from the laundry line or imps would steal the children in the night, because the dragons kept the creatures away.

Of course, those were all just fairy tales...weren't they? Alick thought.

"You realize we're just discussing fairy tales, right?" Rydly voiced what Alick had just been thinking. "Who knows if any of it is true? We could be going on a wild goose chase. Dragons, trolls, imps... they're legend."

"All legends were truth once, Rydly," Alick murmured. "They all have a basis in fact somewhere."

"Alick, we're not discussing some legendary hero, we're discussing mythical creatures!"

"But we *are* discussing legendary heroes, Rydly! The Flame Bringers that settled the land, the ancestors of us all. They believed in the mythical beasts, so maybe they aren't so mythical after all." Alick got up and began to pace, agitated. She was so sure the dragons were real; she couldn't explain it, but she knew they were there somewhere, waiting to be found.

"Alick, this could be a suicide mission," Rydly whispered.

Alick opened her mouth to answer, but Sam beat her to it. "Is it any more suicidal than trying to seize the throne from Fallon alone?" she asked Rydly. "We've been given an opportunity for change, but we can't do it by ourselves. We need help."

"But is running off to find possibly mythical help really the kind of aid we need?" Rydly shot back.

"Who else is going to help us, Rydly?" Karter asked. "The terms of the takeover are clear. Only people from this country are allowed to participate in the war for the crown. The citizens available to help are all middle-aged women, men too old to farm, and children. That's not a formidable army that can take down Fallon."

"What about the men who work on the wall? They're not loyal to Fallon," Rydly ventured.

"Even if we could free them to help, they only number a hundred at most. Fallon's amassed an army of at least six hundred," Sam said, dejectedly.

"If Fallon keeps those hundred, that'll make six hundred trained soldiers and a hundred desperate men against seventy teenagers. I do not like those odds," Karter reasoned.

"This is insane," Rydly muttered.

"Karter and I will leave in the morning." Alick sat back down and started tapping her foot insistently with nervous energy.

"What?" Sam asked. "You two can't go alone."

"Who else would I take, Sam? I need you here with the Pantasmas; we can't leave them without a leader."

"Let Peter be in charge," Rydly said. "Sam and I should go with you too, Alick."

"I wouldn't trust Peter to be in charge of the Pantasmas if my life depended on it."

"Which it could actually, you know, because you don't know what you'll face beyond this forest," Sam murmured. "What if you never come back, Alick?"

Alick grimaced. "I will be back. And that's a promise. I will win this kingdom and save its people if it is the last thing I do."

CHAPTER 23

enolithic rocks began to appear in the forest as Karter and Alick trekked along the path. The packs the two Pantasmas carried were laden with food, water and an extra change of clothes for warmth. The two had set out in the early hours of dawn with the light barely seeping through the canopy.

Sam and Rydly were the only ones who knew that they had left and where they were going. Karter was still uneasy that they hadn't told the Pantasmas about the trip—with Peter chomping at the bit, it seemed a bad idea to give a reason to distrust Alick, and disappearing was a great reason to distrust someone. But Alick said it was better this way. It had been difficult enough to convince Rydly and Sam of their plan, and they trusted Alick implicitly. How would they ever have convinced the rest of the Pantasmas?

As the sun sank toward the horizon, the world around them began to change. They'd spent all day walking in the forest, but now the terrain was gradually becoming dominated by low rocks and shrubs instead of stately trees and vine-like undergrowth.

When Karter had first seen the rocks, he had been amazed; he had never seen xenolithic rocks before. However, the sight quickly grew wearisome after Karter nearly broke his ankle tripping over one of the strange phenomena. If only the nearest road wasn't an entire kingdom away, then they could walk on even ground.

With no map to guide them and the moss of trees no longer available to aid them, Karter and Alick were left to track the sun as they walked to keep to their northern trek. Karter remembered the neat little compass he had had as a child and wondered what had happened to it after he left home, cursing himself for not thinking of taking it with him.

High in the sky, the clouds drifted overhead, and a breeze whistled by, blowing Alick's hair into Karter's face. Karter shook his head and moved out of the way of the whipping strands before they blinded him. Alick shot him an inquisitive look but Karter ignored her, continuing to watch his feet over the uneven terrain. He heard a small thunk and looked behind him, surprised when he saw Alick sitting on a particularly large rock, watching him.

"Why don't we take a break?" she asked, retrieving her water flask and taking a sip. She sounded slightly winded.

"Um... okay." Karter backtracked and sat on a smaller rock across from her. Once he sat, he realized how sore his muscles were. He wasn't entirely sure if he could stand up again.

"Where do you suppose we are?"

Karter shrugged. "Dunno, I never paid much attention to maps in my lessons. Seems silly of me now." He pounded on his calf a couple times in an effort to release a cramp.

Alick gave him a weird look as she drank more water. "Tell me about your childhood," she said, leaning forward slightly.

Karter furrowed his eyebrows. "There aren't really many interesting things to tell."

"Did your parents really not like you?"

Karter gave a harsh laugh. "I'm not even sure my father even acknowledged my brother had a twin. My mother loved me, though, I think. She often fussed over me whenever I caught ill, which was a lot in my youth. As I grew older, I didn't see her as much. I had younger siblings, though. They were sad to see me go."

"It must have been nice having siblings. What are their names?" Alick asked, a longing look coming over her face.

Karter smiled. He had always taken his siblings for granted, but he had to admit he missed them. He couldn't imagine being an only child like Alick, though she did have Sam and Rydly. "Do you want to know their common names or their proper names?"

At that, Alick actually laughed, making Karter feel good inside. Alick didn't laugh enough.

"Tell me their common names. After all, that's what we call each other by."

"Well, my twin never actually went by his common name. Being the heir to the throne, he was only ever referred to as Balthazar except by our mother. She called him Alair."

"So Alair was his common name?"

Karter nodded. "I have four sisters, Kendria, Evelyn, Carleigh, and Lilliana, and another brother, Langley."

"And they're all younger then you?"

Karter nodded. "Kendria's fifteen, Evelyn is ten, Carleigh just turned seven, and Lilliana and Langley are four.

"Are Langley and Lilliana twins too?"

"Not quite, they're ten months apart. Langley was born in March, and Lilliana was born that December."

Alick nodded. She was silent for a while, watching the various bushes move with the breeze. Karter couldn't tell what she was thinking. As he watched her, a particularly strong breeze blew her hair every which way, bringing her back to reality. With a small jerk, she shook her head and looked over at Karter.

"Why are you looking at me like that?" she asked.

"I wasn't looking at you," Karter said quickly, a blush rising up the back of his neck.

"You were," she said, rolling her eyes. "What's your proper name, Karter?" she asked with a sigh, looking at him quizzically.

"What?" Karter feigned deafness.

Alick furrowed her eyebrows. "Your name, Karter. What is your first name? You won't tell me."

Karter opened and closed his mouth like a fish. "I...uh."

"You know my proper name, and Rydly's and Sam's, so what's yours?" Alick pressed the point. She was staring at him now, making Karter very uncomfortable. If she knew his name, she might figure out who he was; she had been noble too, so she might know.

"Karter!"

"Lynton," Karter blurted out loudly and much more harshly than he intended. "My name is Lynton Karter, Karenza."

Alick looked taken aback that he'd used her proper name, and he felt guilty, but he also felt like he'd shared a part of himself that he never should have. No one but the priest had ever called him Lynton, and as it was Karter's proper name, it was something he'd given up with his title upon leaving Outeiro.

Alick got up and walked a few feet away until all Karter could see was her back. "When I was little," she said, "everyone called me Karenza. Even my parents referred to me as Karenza unless it was just the three of us. That night, when—"

Alick broke off, and Karter heard the familiar deep breath Alick took whenever she was about to mention Fallon, as if it pained her to even think about him. He couldn't blame her. He didn't like talking about his past either, and his was significantly less tragic.

"—when Fallon took the castle, I left that name behind. I hadn't heard it until Heritor Day, and I haven't heard it since."

Lynton bowed his head, feeling even guiltier then he had before. "I was never called Lynton. To be called my proper name would mean I meant something, my father said. But I was to be kicked out of the kingdom when I came of age. I was nobody, no matter who my parents were. I left that name behind when I left my kingdom, but I hadn't been called it since I was baptized."

Alick turned around. "Were your younger siblings called by their proper names?"

Karter nodded, recalling the sting he had felt in public, always being called by his common name like a, well, like a commoner. "Like you, my siblings were always called by their proper names in public. I was not afforded that luxury."

"Was it obvious?"

Karter let out a short, harsh laugh. "When your siblings are called Balthazar, Elinor, Adeline, Annabelle, Aidric and Evangeline while you're called Karter, what do you think?" He shook his head, attempting to banish his bitter thoughts. He had sworn a long time ago that it was no good to dwell on the past.

Alick looked at him with an emotion Karter could not identify. It wasn't pity or confusion, but maybe something in between.

"What?" Karter asked, genuinely curious about what she was thinking.

Alick shook her head. "I wonder sometimes which of us had the worse childhood. Me, the orphan who fended for herself in the woods while a monetary reward was placed on her head, or you, when you were ridiculed and placed aside constantly simply because you were small."

"Both of us were victims of circumstance. At least I had a family. You were alone."

Alick smiled sadly. "Just because you had others around you, doesn't mean you weren't alone." She picked up her pack and began moving off again, leaving Karter to scramble up, lost in his thoughts.

CHAPTER 24

ertical cliffs, layered beige and red, with different sedimentary rocks, surrounded Alick as she and Karter walked through a narrow canyon in the foothills of the mountain range. It had taken them two days to walk out of the forest, and five to walk through the inhospitable lowlands that seemed to contain nothing but rocks and low bushes. They hadn't seen a single animal in nearly three days, though Alick could feel their eyes watching every move the two travelers made. They were in wild territory now; Alick knew it was only a matter of time until they met a beast to challenge their path.

"A week beyond the reach of men, creatures of legends lurk," Alick whispered.

"Or so the stories say," Karter muttered back.

Alick smiled despite herself. She and Karter hadn't talked too much during the trip, and though at first Alick had found the silence refreshing, she was quickly starting to yearn for conversation. She was immensely interested by Karter's family, but was conscious that he probably didn't want to talk about them after they'd kicked him out. She'd only brought them up that one day when they'd rested on a particularly large cluster of rock.

The only problem now was what to talk about. So many topics were off limits now. Family, the Pantasmas, Fallon.

All thoughts of conversation were driven out of Alick's head as she and Karter rounded the bend in the canyon and found themselves facing a large oasis. Alick could barely see the other side of the lake where it lapped against the canyon walls. The oasis was not the problem, though. The problem was twofold. First, the canyon walls were still sheer and thus they had reached a dead end and they would have to backtrack again, and second, a large herd of unicorns roamed the pasture between Alick, Karter and the lake.

"They're beautiful," Alick whispered. The pure-white animals grazed, their silvery white spiral horns rising delicately from their foreheads.

"Do you think we can reach the water without being stabbed?" Karter asked.

"Why on earth would they hurt us?" Alick asked back, lulled by the serenity of the valley that was almost surreal in its perfection. Alick began walking closer to the water, almost subconsciously, when a loud shriek like a dying cat wrenched the air.

As one, the glory of Unicorns raised their heads in alarm.

"Alick," Karter said warningly.

"What was that?" Alick whispered back.

"I don't know, but it's scaring them. Back up. Now."

Alick gently took a step backwards, then another, until she was even with Karter again.

"What now?"

But Karter didn't have a chance to answer. The shriek sounded again, closer.

"Run!" Karter yelled; he grabbed Alick's arm and pulled her back toward the ravine as the glory took off.

"We'll never make it, Karter!" Alick screamed. The unicorns were about ten feet away and closing quickly, their horns lowered at a deadly angle, not to mention the possibility of being trampled. Alick lowered her head and doubled her efforts at running, but even then she knew they'd never make it out of the ravine before they were overrun. They both weren't used to such sprinting and their breathing was quickly becoming labored.

"Wait, Alick, this way." Karter grabbed her wrist again and yanked her toward the nearest tree. "Give me your foot," he yelled.

Alick lifted her foot off the ground automatically, then yelped in surprise as Karter threw her into the air toward the tree. Luckily he'd thrown her high enough that she landed on a branch with her stomach, because it wasn't until the bark knocked the wind out of her that she realized what had happened.

Quick as a flash, she hoisted herself into the leaves, coughing slightly from the impact and looked down to see where the unicorns were.

She gasped. "Hurry!" she screamed hoarsely at Karter, her breathing quickening in alarm. The thunderous sound of the hooves was nearly deafening now. Karter jumped as high as he could and managed to grab the branch with one hand.

"I've got you," Alick screamed, grabbing his other hand and guiding it toward the branch. The unicorns would be beneath the tree in seconds.

"Swing up! Swing up!" Alick watched as Karter swung his legs up toward the tree branch, hooking them. But before he could pull his back up, the first of the unicorns passed underneath the tree, its horn up in the air.

Alick heard, rather than saw, the sound of ripping fabric shortly before Karter howled in pain and jerked up to meet the branch with his stomach. Alick reached out to help him on top of the branch and flinched when she felt his blood running down her arm.

Karter's breathing was ragged, his face drawn in pain, but they were both safe as long as they could hold onto the tree. Alick looked down in wonder at the sea of white running beneath her, shuddering at how close they'd come to being underneath the moving mass, trampled.

"Alick," Karter gasped. Alick looked back up and saw that Karter had turned his back toward to her.

Alick, too, gasped in horror at the bleeding gash that ran down Karter's back, exposing muscle and ligament, and dripping in crimson.

"Is it that bad?" Karter asked weakly.

"You'll be fine," Alick said, more to reassure herself than anything. There was a lot of blood. "It missed your spine," Alick added. But before she could examine the wound further, the injured cat shriek sounded again.

"What is that?" Alick asked, gripping the tree for support as she strained to see the source of the noise.

Karter didn't say anything; he just pointed toward the top of the valley where a shape was coming into focus.

Alick peered through the branches in wonder as the shape came into focus.

"Karter, is that what I think it is?" Alick asked, half in wonder, half in fear.

"A griffin." Karter's voice was nearly lost among the noise of the stampede below, and Alick had to strain to hear him.

"Are we safe here?"

"I don't think it's after us."

Alick watched as the griffin swooped down, following the unicorns into the ravine. As it passed, Alick got a brief glimpse of its curved beak and tawny hide. At the entrance to the ravine, it dropped to the ground, tucked in its great wing span and began to run on its lion legs after the unicorns.

"Will they be okay?" Alick strained to see through the ravine, almost falling out of the tree.

"We almost got trampled by a glory of unicorns as they fled in fear of a griffin, and you're concerned about the unicorns?!" Karter asked incredulously.

Alick ducked her head and smiled sheepishly. "Sorry," she muttered. She couldn't help, however, but wait for the dreaded sound of the griffin's claws ripping through the unicorns. Luckily, it never came. Or at least it happened far enough away that she couldn't hear it.

Together they sat there and listened as the unicorns' hooves and griffin's shrieks faded into the distance, leaving the valley as quiet as when Alick and Karter had first found it.

"Come on," Alick said, dropping down from the tree. "I think it's safe now."

Alick watched as Karter carefully lowered himself out of the tree, his biceps bulging as he held up his full weight for a few moments before dropping do the ground with a small cry of pain.

"We need to clean that gash before we move on."

"Why don't we stay here for the night?" Karter asked.

"I'm not sure it's safe."

"The valley's safer than the ridge."

"Except for all the creatures that probably come to drink."

"Point taken. We'll sleep as far away from the water as we can in the valley."

Alick smiled and then quickly ducked her head so Karter wouldn't notice.

"We'll discuss this after I clean that gash."

"I can clean my own injuries."

"It's on your back. Good luck with that." Alick rolled her eyes. "Now give me your shirt."

Karter narrowed his eyes at her, but did as she asked, wincing as he peeled the fabric away from the rapidly drying blood.

Alick took it from him and proceeded to the water's edge.

"What are you doing?"

"Using it as a rag."

"Hey, I have to wear that."

"It's practically ripped in half, I'm pretty sure the only thing keeping it on you was the blood," Alick said, rolling her eyes again. She walked back over toward Karter with the wet shirt and proceeded to clean the wound. She had to keep pretending it wasn't a big deal. If she did that, she wouldn't panic. She couldn't panic.

"Ouch, watch it," Karter yelped as Alick accidentally pressed too hard.

"I have to apply *some* pressure, it's still bleeding."

"How deep is it?"

"Deep enough that it could probably use stitches."

"I am *not* letting you stitch up my back."

"Gee, thanks."

"I wouldn't let anyone without a medical background stitch up my back."

"Thanks for the clarification, but it doesn't really matter. I have nothing to stitch it up with anyway."

Karter let out a relieved sigh.

"No need to sound happy," Alick grumbled. "You're going to have a wicked scar instead."

"Maybe it will be impressive."

Alick rolled her eyes, but she was smiling. She was glad Karter was still in good spirits. The gash on his back was nearly a foot long and at least half an inch deep at its shallowest point. They'd have to be careful it didn't get infected. Alick went back to the water to rinse out the shirt and happened to catch a glimpse of Karter's bare chest.

The blush was almost immediate, and Alick wondered why she was embarrassed. She had seen most of the Pantasmas shirtless at one point or another. But in the back of Alick's mind, there was the niggling idea that the Pantasmas were family. Alick shook her head. Karter was a Pantasma too. There was no need to feel embarrassed about seeing his abs.

Once the shirt resembled white again, Alick walked back over to Karter and recommenced attempting to both stop the bleeding and clean the wound.

"Thank you," Karter said after three more trips to the lake and back.

"For what?"

"Taking care of me."

"What kind of travel buddy would I be if I let you die of an infection?"

Karter was silent for a long while. "Well thanks," he said quietly.

Alick paused in her cleaning and looked down at the grass, suddenly very conscious of how close she was to Karter. "You're welcome," she whispered back. She surveyed his back, which was now relatively blood free.

"We're going to need a bandage," she said at normal volume again.

"Might as well rip up the shirt," Karter said. "It's already got one tear."

Alick nodded and began rip said shirt into strips long enough to wrap around Karter's abdomen. Alick picked up the various strips and began wrapping them around Karter's chest, trying not to pay attention to Karter as he winced with every knot, but it was difficult.

"Sorry," she said as she pulled one strip particularly tight to get it to knot, causing Karter to yelp.

"It's fine," Karter said, turning his head toward her as he spoke so when Alick looked up from tying another knot, he was mere inches away.

Alick gulped. She had never been so close to him before. She stared into Karter's hazel eyes, her chest beating so rapidly she was surprised Karter couldn't hear it. Karter turned his head slightly to the side and gave her a small smile. Alick could have sworn she began hyperventilating. She quickly tied the last knot and stood up.

She looked up into the sky and saw the sun was almost to the horizon. Alick hadn't realized how long it had taken her to cleanse Karter's gash.

"We'd best find somewhere to spend the night," Karter piped up from the ground.

Alick nodded. "And somewhere hidden. We don't want any visits from wild animals during the night."

"Though finding one for dinner wouldn't be amiss."

"Karter!" Alick exclaimed.

"I was kidding," Karter replied indignantly. "Unicorns taste terrible anyway."

CHAPTER 25

Yesterday had sucked. Today sucked. Tomorrow would probably suck too. The mountain rocks pierced Karter's feet with every step, the sun beat down on his neck, sweat made his hair stick uncomfortably to his forehead, and to top it all off, every step sent shooting pain up Karter's back where the unicorn had grazed him. The sun and sweat, Karter could live with. He'd learned to tolerate them on the long road from Outeiro to Conquistado. Constant pain, however, was a new experience.

Not that Karter could show his pain. The entire morning, Alick had turned around every other step up the steep mountainside to make sure he was okay. Finally, Karter had insisted on going first so that Alick wouldn't trip and fall up the mountain in her concern for him. If he so much as winced, Alick started insisting that they stop, but Karter refused to hold up Alick's mission. He had volunteered to come on this quest, and it wouldn't be right if he slowed her down. If that meant bottling up his pain, then that is what he would do.

The mountainside was so steep at this point, Alick and Karter were virtually scaling the side, not walking.

"Do you suppose it will ever level out again, Karter?" Alick huffed from below him.

Karter looked down and was surprised to saw Alick plastered to the rock, most of her blonde hair hanging loose from her ponytail and caked to her head and neck from perspiration. Her forehead was beginning to turn pink with sun, but her bright blue eyes were clear as Alick met Karter's eyes with defiance, daring him to say no.

Karter looked back up the mountainside, straining to see something that resembled a ledge they could rest on, but there was nothing but sheer rock.

"I don't think we'll get rest for a while yet, Alick," Karter said grimly.

"Ugh," Alick groaned. "Surely there was an easier path up the ridge."

Karter smiled to himself. He couldn't help it. There was something so surreal about their journey. The longer they travelled, the more the Pantasmas and the threat Fallon posed to them seemed like a dream. But their destination didn't feel any more real. What felt real was the endless wandering, the desire to keep going forward toward an unknown end with the slim hope that what they would find might be worthwhile. What felt real was the pain of the day and the fright of the night, the whispers that seemed to follow them, and the conversations they carried.

What felt real was Alick.

Karter was so caught up in his thoughts that he didn't notice the top of the mountain ridge until he was falling over it.

"Karter!"

Karter dimly heard Alick shriek his name as he fell with a thud onto solid rock.

"Karter, Karter, answer me." He felt Alick shaking him and opened an eye.

"Am I dead?"

"Not yet, Karter. Not yet." Alick smiled.

"Suppose I should've been paying more attention to where I was climbing," Karter winced.

"I wasn't paying any attention either until I saw you disappear. I was too busy focusing on the lack of feeling in my arms and legs."

"Hah, I'm not sure I even know what those are anymore." Karter gently rolled up to a sitting position and looked around him.

The mountainside they'd been climbing ended with a sharp edge, immediately dropping down to the rock they now lay on five feet below.

"It's such a perfect end to the mountain, like someone purposefully took a cleaver to it," Alick muttered.

"Or some*thing*," Karter said, standing to inspect the edge just above his head. "But you're right, normal mountains don't suddenly reach a perfect peak and then drop right back down. Do they?"

"Not in my experience."

Karter shook his head and looked around. This side of the mountain was mostly a large, flat plateau with a shimmering lake. It truly did look like someone had scooped out a chunk of the mountain. To their left, a small path led up into what remained of the mountain.

"Well, which way, your majesty?"

"What?" Alick made a small strangled yelp and looked at him like she'd seen a ghost.

"What?" Karter said.

"You called me 'your majesty'."

"So?"

"So, I'm no majesty."

Karter rolled his eyes. "It was an expression, Alick. Besides, if we beat Fallon, you *will* be queen."

"Right," Alick murmured. But Karter could tell she wasn't really paying attention to him anymore; she was focused on a memory.

Karter shrugged and began walking off toward the lake. They needed more water, and surely a lake this high up would be sanitary. Alick trailed behind him, still looking troubled, making Karter wonder why exactly she had reacted so adversely to being called "your majesty". Part of Karter said, *It's because* you *called her that,* while the other part of him thought that was absurd. Why would Alick care what Karter thought?

The lake was large and still but clear in the shallows, so Karter began removing his bandage to cleanse the wound beneath.

"Here, let me help," Alick said gently.

Karter ceased attempting to untie his bandages and simply sat, listening to the wind and water as Alick removed each of the strips of cloth and washed them on the rocks letting all the blood seep away into the lake.

"Perhaps we should have filled our water first. Then washed the blood into the lake."

Alick smiled tiredly at Karter, and he couldn't help but smile back. She looked especially beautiful with the setting sun illuminating her from behind, but he couldn't tell her that.

Karter began concentrating on the ripples of water instead so he wouldn't accidentally slip up and tell Alick his thoughts. However, as Karter stared at the water, he noticed that the ripples emanating from the washed bandages were meeting with other ripples.

Karter looked around, but there was nothing else around the lake to cause them.

"Hey, Alick?" Karter started, beginning to get uneasy.

But before he could say anything, something shot out of the water and grabbed Alick's leg, pulling her to the ground and out into the water so quickly she didn't even have time to scream.

"Alick!" Karter grabbed her hand just before she was pulled under and managed to pull her up to shore, but whatever had hold of her was not giving up so easily. A second something shot out and grabbed Alick's other leg, exerting more force to pull Alick down to the depths. This time, though, Karter was prepared enough to grab Alick's other hand and pull back with all his might, keeping the two of them on dry land for the moment.

"What is it?!" Alick yelled.

Karter tilted his head to see Alick's legs and felt his stomach drop like a stone. Wrapped around Alick's legs were two tentacles like those from an octopus, pale pink and covered in small suction-cups.

"Karter, what has me?" Alick demanded.

"Tentacles," Karter gasped. It was taking all of his strength to keep Alick from being dragged into the water and down into the mouth of whatever this new attacker was. He had to think of something quick. Alick was already beginning to grimace in pain from being used as a tug of war rope by Karter and the tentacled creature.

"Alick. Alick grab my leg."

"What?!"

"I can't fight this thing and hold you at the same time, grab my legs."

Karter abruptly sat down, transferring Alick's grip from his hands to his calves, his seated position helping him maintain some leverage over the tentacles.

"What are you doing, Karter?" Alick gasped as they slid toward the water by a fraction of an inch.

Karter reached above his head and was just able to grab Alick's bow and quiver from their packs.

"Karter?" Alick said again, sounding distressed. They were continuing to slide toward the lake.

"I've got this, Alick."

Alick's feet were almost underwater at this point, and Karter was finding it difficult to concentrate on where he was shooting with Alick screaming at him to hurry.

Karter drew his arm back and aimed where he believed the tentacles to be and released the string. The familiar zing of the bow sounded and a dull thunk shortly followed before an ear-piercing inhuman scream filled the air and the water erupted with tentacles, the two holding Alick releasing her and shooting up into the air to join their brethren. Karter grabbed his short sword and severed the tentacle aimed at his waist. Meanwhile, Alick scrambled up the bank behind him and grabbed her bow and quiver that Karter had dropped when the creature screamed.

Karter cut off another tentacle and backed up from the water, all the while the screams continued, sounding like cats being trampled.

"Alick! Run!" Karter yelled. The creature was clearly aquatic, and they had to get out of its reach.

Karter glanced back and saw Alick standing with her bow, shooting arrows at any appendage that moved; she couldn't see the tentacle that was about to whack her from the back.

"Alick!" Karter screamed. He lunged at her and knocked her down just as the tentacle ripped through where she had just been.

"Karter?" Alick asked, seeming disoriented at their sudden vantage point.

"Run!" Karter replied pushing her toward the mountain. He turned around and continued hacking at various limbs as he ran backward, praying he wouldn't trip on anything. It didn't take long to be out of reach of the tentacles, but Karter and Alick didn't stop. They were being fueled by fear and desperation that flooded the body like a broken dam overwhelms a river. And so they kept running, faster and faster and faster toward the mountain path and whatever lay beyond.

CHAPTER 26

Just as Alick and Karter cleared the first bend of the mountain's pass, hundreds of miles away, back in the Rebel Forest, Sam and Rydly were attempting to control the Pantasmas.

"I'm telling you, Fallon's men are too close. We need to start picking them off or they could find us!" Peter argued again.

"And I'm telling *you*, Peter, that that's a stupid idea," Sam seethed. "If Fallon's men start disappearing, don't you think he'll come looking for them?"

"Fallon doesn't care about his men, why would he come?"

"Because he'd know that we're responsible! Honestly, you're the strategic genius, why are you so dense today?" Sam rolled her eyes and turned her back on Peter. "We stay hidden. Alick's orders. When she gets back, we need an army, not scraps. Keep up their training."

"How do you even know she'll return?" Peter spat back.

"I have faith in her, even if you don't."

"Don't let your friendship blind you. Alick's abandoned us with her new pet."

"Karter is not a pet, and Alick would never abandon her people. *She* has honor."

"Oh, and I don't?"

"You are a different sort of person, Peter, cold and ruthless when it comes to military. You'd kill the lot of us without a second thought if you thought it would give you the advantage on the battlefield." The two were facing each other across the table now, bright red and angry as they fought.

"I leave you two alone for two minutes and you're on the verge of killing each other again."

Rydly entered the tent, immediately ending the argument. Sam and Peter both composed themselves and, with a baleful look, Peter left the tent, saying as he left, "The Pantasmas can't take much more training, Samantha. They're going to collapse from exhaustion before long."

"Why must you antagonize everyone so?" Rydly asked Sam with a sigh as he set down the roll of papers he had been holding.

"Not my fault he's lacking a brain," Sam said defensively as she opened up the first paper. "What's this?"

"Latest surveillance from Peter's spies. Locations of Fallon's troops, supplies, et cetera."

"They're closing in."

Rydly nodded. "I don't know if it's coincidence or if he knows we're here, but the wall comes closer every day. They're starting to store their supplies on the outside of the wall instead of the inside, bringing them right to our doorstep."

"Should we move again?" Sam asked.

"Hold everything. Did *you* just ask *me* for *advice*?" Rydly mocked. Sam narrowed her eyes and gave Rydly a small shove in the chest.

"I can't make all the decisions," she said quietly, looking down at the maps. "There is too much at stake."

Rydly put his hand over hers and looked her straight in the eye. "Alick *will* come back. She *will* survive."

Sam bit her lip. "You heard that part of the argument, huh?" she asked Rydly.

Rydly shook his head. "I didn't hear any of your argument with Peter. I just know you." He patted her hand and moved around the table, shuffling through the papers as he went.

Sam watched him, wondering when Rydly had grown up.

That night, the Pantasmas moved camp again, retreating deeper into the Rebel Forest. Before going to bed, both Sam and Rydly prayed to the stars that Alick would return soon, safe and sound. They needed her.

CHAPTER 27

"Look at this, Karter!" Alick called to Karter's retreating figure. Alick went up to the design in the rock face that she had seen, running her hand over the grooved lines. She heard Karter's footsteps behind her and turned.

"Look," she repeated, holding her Crista Real next to the design.

"They're the same," Karter said in wonder, taking the Crista Real from Alick and comparing them. Alick watched him, his hair sticking up at odd angles, dried blood streaking his clothing that they hadn't been able to wash. She probably looked no better, though her largest injury had caused no blood. As Karter continued to compare the two designs, Alick sat down on a nearby rock and rubbed her swollen ankle. She had insisted on

Karter going in front so he wouldn't see how badly she was limping and insist on stopping.

In her preoccupation with her ankle, Alick didn't realize Karter was staring at her until he knelt down by her foot.

"What happened?" he asked, sounding equally gentle and horrified as he examined the bruising and swelling.

"Nothing, I'm fine." Alick yanked her foot back from him and then gasped from the pain it caused.

"You are not fine," Karter replied firmly, taking her foot again. "Now what happened; did you trip?"

Alick shook her head. "It was that tentacled creature, when it grabbed me yesterday."

"We need to take care of this. Try and relax." Karter moved off, presumedly to get something from their meager supplies to bind her ankle.

"Karter, we don't have time for this. We have to keep moving." Alick stood back up and hobbled over to the design. "What do you suppose this means?"

Karter came over and gently pushed her back to the ground. "I think it means we're close. Which means dragons, which means you need to be able to run."

Alick sighed. "I suppose you're right."

"Generally, that is true," Karter said with a small smile.

Alick laughed and shoved his shoulder playfully.

"That's good," Karter said. "Keep laughing. It will distract you."

"Distract me from what?" Alick said before pain shot up her leg like a lightning bolt.

"That," Karter said simply as he continued bandaging her ankle.

Alick glared at him.

"Hey, you caused me just as much pain caring for my back."

"Uh, that is unfair. I was as gentle as I could be."

"I am too!"

"You are not," Alick protested as he tightened the bandage one final time.

Karter's reply was interrupted by an ominous rumble in the distance.

"What was that?" Alick asked, looking up into the sky. She stood up and moved so that she could see more of the sky. "Those clouds don't look very friendly," she said as pitch black thunderclouds began to move into view. A drop of water fell on Alick's wrist and as she looked at it, more and more began coming down as the wind began to pick up. Alick looked at Karter, feeling uneasy.

"We don't want to be out in his storm, do we?" Karter asked.

Alick shook her head. "No, this one I think we'll need to sit out. Come on, let's find a cave or something, quick." Alick grabbed the nearest pack and began to move off, jerking to a halt when Karter grabbed the handle on her back.

"Take this one," he said, handing her the smaller of the two and taking the one off her back.

"I am perfectly capable of carrying the big one, thank you very much." Alick protested, slapping his hand.

Karter shook his head. "The less weight you carry, the faster that ankle will heal. Now come on."

Alick huffed and followed him. Since coming to the Pantasmas, Karter had really grown up. She wasn't used to being taken care of. She'd been the carer for over a decade; Sam often tried, but Alick could always convince her that she was fine. Karter saw right through her.

"How's this?" Karter asked Alick as they came across a shallow cave. She was still too far behind him to see inside it, but she could tell it was the closest thing to shelter for a while.

"Is it deep enough to start a fire in this?" Alick gestured toward the sheets of rain that were coming at them sideways. The two travelers were practically yelling to be heard over the wind that whipped through the mountain pass.

"Pretty sure."

"Then let's go." Alick pushed past Karter into the back of the cave and practically threw her pack on the ground. She rested for a brief moment and then dragged herself to her feet, taking stock of the cave. It was on the shallow side, allowing Karter and Alick to see that they were alone and no animal called the space home. Thank goodness for small favors.

Karter was busy digging through the packs for burnable material while Alick explored the area. By the time a spark was going, the storm outside was raging full force, with tornado-grade winds, sheets of rain, and thunder and lightning loud enough to deafen. Between the fire and the near constant lightning flash, light wasn't a problem. Alick just prayed the wind wouldn't turn the other way and start blowing the rain into the cave instead of away from it.

"How long do you suppose we'll be in here?" she asked, sitting down by the fire to warm herself and dry her clothing. The rain had really dropped the temperature.

Karter shrugged his shoulders and then shook his wet hair like a dog before answering, "I have a feeling we'll be here all night."

Alick pursed her lips and looked at the unfriendly rock walls around them. "Not a very cozy spot," she commented wryly, annoyed at the delay.

Karter shrugged, "If you ignore the pointy rocks, it's not so bad."

"Karter, the entire cave is pointy rocks."

"Well, yeah..."

Alick couldn't help but laugh quietly.

"I like it when you laugh," Karter said suddenly, surprising Alick. "It's a pretty sound."

Alick ducked her head, feeling herself blush. "Thanks," she replied, staring resolutely at the fire as a smile danced across her face. "Will you tell me more about your siblings?" Alick asked as the silence began to grow uncomfortable.

Karter looked at her. "What do you want to know?"

"What did you do all day; what did you play? Did you often travel?" Alick leaned closer to the fire to warm her hands, watching Karter for his reaction. He looked taken aback at the questions, but quickly that look was replaced by one of nostalgia as he began to tell her of his childhood.

He described days that were filled with playing hide and seek through the castle, picnics to the seaside where he and his sisters would run in the sand and sea spray. He described the days and days he spent in lessons, always learning from books, never allowed to take part in sword play, forced to watch as his brother moved up through the ranks of the knights until he was the general of all his father's armies, the perfect position for the future king. Karter lapsed into silence, leaving only the pounding rain and residual thunder claps.

Alick moved to sit next to Karter and took his hand, not being able to bear him looking so sad. "When I was little," she said to distract him, "my mother and father took me to this gorgeous spot at the far edge of our kingdom where a waterfall meets a small pool with smooth stones and crystal-clear water." Alick smiled, remembering the day. "The sky was the brightest blue I think I've ever seen. The plant life was so green and alive I could believe they were magic. I played there all day, the waterfall rushing down, not unlike this rain." Alick stopped, the memory broken.

She looked at Karter, who was still staring at the fire, not quite hearing her. She turned toward him more and held his hand with both of hers, causing him to look up into her eyes with a question burning in them. Alick smiled and looked back into the fire, letting herself be reabsorbed into her story.

"We had a picnic right there by the water. It was just sandwiches, nothing too special. I finished quickly and was capering about, swimming around, when a fish brushed up against my leg. I screamed and ran out of the water right into my father's arms, traumatized." Alick laughed at her childhood folly and was rewarded by a small chuckle from Karter as well. Alick's smile dropped as she remembered the rest, the nostalgia of being so cared for causing pains in her heart.

"My father held me in his arms and laughed. He said, 'My dear, Alick, my little brave Alick. You cannot be scared of a little fish. Life will throw so many more things at you as you grow, things that will terrify you to bits. But you must never give into fear. Bravery is being able to conquer your fears. You must promise me you will be the bravest girl to ever live, Alick. Promise me that.'" Alick cut off, tears springing to her eyes. All these years later, it was still hard to remember her family. "I wonder if he knew," she started, but Karter cut her off.

"Shhh," he said, putting his arms around her. "It's all right."

Alick gave a small laugh. "And here I was trying to comfort you."

She felt Karter smile, and he pulled back just enough that he could look her in the eyes. "Well, now it's my turn," he said. "Alick, your father would be so proud of you right now."

"Sitting in a cave in the night with a raging storm outside accompanied only by a boy my age?" Alick asked nervously, attempting to ease the tension she felt between them. She was ever conscious of the fact that Karter's lips were scarcely three inches away.

Karter smiled and leaned a little closer. "No, Alick, because of the brave, brave person you have become. You're a brilliant leader."

Alick's breath caught in her throat and she leaned even closer to Karter so that their foreheads were touching, their eyes locked on each other. Alick couldn't help but think how absolutely beautiful they were, gray-green with little blue flecks.

A particularly loud thunderclap sounded, startling Alick. She jumped back, tipping over and nearly sticking her foot in the fire.

"Are you all right?" Karter asked urgently, helping her back to a sitting position.

"Um yeah, I'm fine, we should, uh, probably get some sleep," Alick muttered as she stood up, brushed herself off, and moved over to retrieve a blanket from the packs. If she had bothered to look back at Karter, she would have seen the momentary look of disappointment that flickered across his face, but Alick was too flustered to think of anything besides wanting to be alone to sort out her thoughts. Alick was familiar with a lot of things, but romantic love was not one of them. She only knew how to love her friends, who were more like family. She didn't understand the butterflies that commanded her now. Part of her wished they would go away and stay away. The unknown is a frightening thing and Alick didn't need any more unknowns in her life.

CHAPTER 28

Up and up and up the mountain pass went for days and days on end, until Karter could've sworn they were above the clouds. Neither he nor Alick had brought up that night in the cave and had scarcely spoken to each other since. Between the lack of conversation, the long, hard days, and the rapidly cooling thin air, Karter was ready to give up. If it hadn't been for the symbols carved into the rocks every now and then, they might have.

"There's another one," Karter panted as they reached another bend in the pass. He pointed to the outlines in the rock that matched Alick's trinket perfectly.

"I wonder why they're here," Alick muttered, sounding absent-minded.

"One of your ancestors probably thought someone might want to find the dragons again someday."

Alick didn't reply. Karter kicked a rock in frustration. He didn't understand why Alick was giving him the silent treatment, or why she seemed more preoccupied then usual. He wanted to blame it on the pain of her ankle and the impending dragons, but he worried it was because of him.

"So, do you suppose we're close?" Karter asked, catching up to Alick so they were walking side by side.

Alick didn't seem to hear him.

"Alick? Alick!"

"What?" Alick turned toward him, her eyes far away.

"Are you all right?" Karter asked, concerned.

Alick nodded. "I'm fine, just thinking."

"About what?"

"Starting to think maybe this wasn't the best idea."

Karter couldn't help it. He snorted.

That woke Alick up out of whatever trance she was in.

"Excuse me?" she asked, her voice getting higher. Karter turned so he was walking backwards, looking at her.

"I'm sorry, It's just we're hundreds of miles from home, following markings on an old trail, and now, *now,* you start thinking maybe we shouldn't be stalking ageless creatures who could burn us to a crisp on sight?" Karter laughed and turned back around.

"Hey, you seemed pretty bent on coming with me."

"Well, I couldn't let you get burnt to a crisp without me, could I?" Karter smiled and turned his head to see the indignation he knew would be on Alick's face. And that's why he didn't see the ledge.

The next thing Karter was aware of was falling, crashing, tumbling, vaguely aware of Alick falling with him after she had tried to save him and ended up being pulled over the edge with him. Together, they bumped and bruised themselves all the way down the slope, until, at last, they came to an aching stop, Alick on top of Karter. As Alick rolled off, Karter was able to stir, checking each of his limbs for pains and breaks.

Suddenly, a vise-like grip made him cry out.

"Shhh!" Alick hissed. Karter realized it was her hand gripping his.

"Karter, get up very, very slowly," she whispered, fear filling her voice. That couldn't be good. There wasn't much that frightened Alick.

Karter lifted his head, and his jaw dropped. They hadn't fallen off of a cliff. They'd fallen right into the dragon's nest.

Karter blinked rapidly, but it did not change the view. Dragons. Dragons upon dragons were looking at them, hissing at them, from every angle, every space. They were everywhere. Karter got to his feet, and he and Alick surveyed the space, clinging to each other for all they were worth.

"Now what?" Karter asked. The nest was like a bowl, littered with bones of dead animals with holes in the sides where the dragons slept. As Karter looked, he saw dragons of almost every color and size, from red to black to purple to yellow, from dragons as large as houses to dragons as large as the castle. Each one clinging to the rock and writhing like the snakes they were related to.

"I have absolutely no idea," Alick gasped. Karter could feel her beginning to panic. "I thought we'd have time to make a plan, a point of action—" Alick's words broke off as one of the dragons let out a roar and charged.

"Duck!" Karter pushed Alick off to one side and dove to the other, hitting the ground just as the dragon reached them. It stopped, looked at the two fallen travelers, then lunged for Karter, picked him up with a claw, and took to the skies.

"Karter!"

Alick's scream reverberated around the nest, but the dragon kept flying higher and higher with Karter held tight in its grasp. Karter struggled mightily, trying to loosen the grip so that he could breathe easier and maybe escape if it got closer to the ground, but the claws were like iron, cold and unmoving.

The dragon landed on the highest peak and held Karter up over the edge, and, even though Karter had no idea what the dragons continued roars said, the meaning was clear enough. It intended to drop him.

The one advantage of being almost dashed to pieces by a dragon was that from this high up, Karter could clearly see what was going on below.

Alick was running back and forth, screaming his name, demanding the dragons let him go. Her frustration at being helpless to save him was evident, despite the distance. And in that instant, Karter realized why she'd been avoiding him. He was one more thing she could lose. One more friend that could die.

"Alick, just run!" Karter shouted. The dragon snorted, clearly annoyed he had spoken, and shook him up and down several times.

"Karter!" Alick screamed again. Karter looked down just in time to see Alick dodge a fiery blaze. As she rolled out of the way, putting out the smoldering patches on her clothing, another dragon aimed a blast right for her. She was trying to formulate a plan, but she had to leave; she didn't have time to plan.

"Alick!" Karter screamed. "Run! Leave me!" The dragon holding Karter tightened its grip, leaving Karter gasping for any air he could, unable to form words. Below, the dragons were still firing at Alick, but she wasn't running, she was looking for something. "Alick," Karter gasped, too quietly even for the dragon to hear. Suddenly Alick dove for something, right under a line of fire.

Karter struggled; he had to see if she was okay. But he couldn't see Alick through the smoke and fire that littered the floor of the stone nest.

But suddenly he could hear her voice. Karter felt relief spread through him as Alick appeared at the base of the side where the dragon was holding him, her Crista Real held high.

"What are you doing, Alick?" Karter strained. "Run!" But he knew she could never hear him, not when his windpipe was being crushed.

"My name is Alick Karenza Daveney! Descendent of Feorus the Firebringer, who was your friend. Behold the talisman, forged from dragon claw by dragon fire right here in this mountain! Look at it!"

Karter watched as Alick made her speech, awed by her bravery, standing in the midst of a blaze, trying to reason with dragons.

"We are your friends! Let him go!"

The dragons writhed and hissed at this command, turning amongst themselves, snorting fire and smoke as they all turned toward one particularly large cave.

As Karter watched, a dragon approached from the cave, quickly followed by another. The first one was smallish, bright blue, with green spikes and bright green eyes. The second was bright, fire red with black spikes, large and terrifying to behold.

"I am Alick, defender of the people, descendent of Feoras the Firebringer through his son Favian the Fearless. I carry the talisman forged with claw and fire, a symbol of friendship and bravery. Help me. Help us. Libre has fallen; we must take her back. Release my friend and come to our aid."

"Alick, no," Karter struggled again helplessly as the smaller dragon took to the air, heading straight down for Alick. "Run," he whispered, but Alick held her ground, her fierce expression never wavering, the Crista Real held high as the dragon landed right in front of her, breathing smoke and ash.

"Help me," Alick said again, refusing to back down.

The dragon bent down and looked Alick right in the eye as Karter held his breath. At such close range, Alick would never be able to survive if the dragon decided to attack. After what felt like days, the dragon stretched its neck into the sky and let out a stream of fire, straight up, and then bowed down before Alick.

As Karter watched, one by one, all the dragons in the nest began to do the same, bowing down before the girl in the tattered, singed, clothes who'd held her ground. The dragon holding Karter loosened its grip slightly and flew him back to the ground. When they landed, the dragon let go completely and Karter wasted no time in running to Alick, who threw her arms around him.

"I thought I'd lost you," she gasped.

"You thought you'd lost me?" Karter asked, amazed. "What about you, dragon tamer?" Karter shook his head in amazement at the dragons bowing down before them. "I can't believe we did it."

"*We*?" Alick asked raising her eyebrows.

Karter smiled. "Well, it was all you, but I was still here. And I was worried about you."

"I can take care of myself," Alick said softly, smiling from relief and amazement at the dragons.

Karter took her hand. "So can I, but I always want you watching my back."

Karter smiled again as he watched the blush creep up her cheeks. "Now. Which dragon do you want?" he asked her.

"What?" Alick asked.

"Which dragon do you want?" he asked.

"Uh..." As if the dragons had been listening the blue dragon who had first accepted Alick rose back up and turned sideways, offering her foreleg. "Well, I guess this one," Alick said, scrambling up onto the blue dragons back.

"You should take the red one, Karter," Alick shouted down.

"What? The one with the murderous glare?" Karter asked, incredulous. The dragon in question snorted indignantly and marched over, grabbed Karter with his teeth, and flung him up onto its back.

"I think he likes you," Alick said with a laugh as Karter situated himself upright on the dragon's back.

Karter narrowed his eyes in her general direction. "Haha, very funny."

"It is, actually."

"Okay, maybe... How do you make them go —" Karter cut off as his dragon launched itself into the air with Alick's shortly behind.

Karter heard Alick give an exhilarated laugh and a shout— "Fallon, here we come!" Then all he could hear was the rush of wind as they flew back to Rebel Forest. It had worked. Alick had done it. They had dragons.

CHAPTER 29

The ground sped past beneath Alick as the dragons soared through the sky. What had taken Alick and Karter weeks to travel was quickly passing by in a matter of hours. Riding a dragon wasn't nearly as difficult as Alick thought it was going to be. It was very much like riding a horse, just with variances in height instead of speed. As they began to pass over the outskirts of Rebel Forest, Alick did a loop-the-loop, laughing out loud and whooping with joy.

With such grand beasts on their side, creatures for whom distance was nothing and an acre of forest could burn in an instant, Alick had never felt better about their chances of survival. Alick looked beside her, where Karter was sitting as if he'd been riding dragons his whole life. Alick smiled. It was so hard to feel any stress or worry, danger or fear when they were flying as high as mountains, free as air, with endless possibilities spreading out before them. For the first time, Alick began to wonder about her future. If she became Queen, what would she do? How would she fix the kingdom?

"Karter! Let's stop here!" Alick yelled as soon as she caught sight of the great tree. Alick looked over to see if he'd heard and caught him holding his hand to his ear. Alick waved wildly to get his attention then pointed down several times before beginning to descend. Together, the two dragons glided peacefully through the canopy, coming to rest in a clearing just big enough for the two of them.

"Why'd we stop, Alick?" Karter asked, sliding off his dragon and coming within earshot. "If we land here, it's at least another day's walk to the camp."

"I don't want the dragons to be seen yet, and especially not by Fallon's men."

"You think they're still patrolling the wood?"

"They'd be stupid if they weren't." Alick looked around, out of habit. Now that she was back in her forest, her survival instincts were beginning to reappear. The agitation, stress, and paranoia of being a Pantasma were returning with a vengeance.

"Do you suppose they'll just stay here?" Karter broke through Alick's reverie.

Alick walked over to join him in front of the two dragons. As they stood there, the blue dragon lowered herself to the ground and began to rest, watching them with one large green eye.

"They're pretty smart," Alick said with a shrug. "Maybe they'll listen."

"What if they don't?"

"Well, it's worth a try." Alick grumbled. She knelt by the blue dragon and laid her hand on its nose. "Stay here," she said. "Stay hidden. When I whistle like this—" Alick let out the same piercing whistle she used to keep the Pantasmas in line, "—come to me." The dragon snorted in what Alick hoped was understanding.

"All right, let's go."

"You're not going to tell the other one?" Karter asked, gesturing to his red dragon, standing upright and alert as if on guard.

Alick shook her head no. "I have a feeling she's in charge." Alick pointed to the blue dragon. "He won't go anywhere without her."

"You think this'll work?" Karter asked.

Alick took a deep breath. "It has to," she said simply. And then the two set off into the woods, making for the Pantasma camp.

The sun was beginning to sink in the sky by the time Alick and Karter found a recognizable path. "We're not as far away as I thought," Alick murmured as she looked around. The wood was thinner than when they'd last been there, the leaves turning brilliant colors and dropping to the forest floor.

The "path" Alick and Karter were following wasn't really a path at all; the Pantasmas had long since decided that having a path to their camp was too dangerous. Instead, they memorized forest landmarks: which trees had moss, which trees had fallen, which trees had holes where animals lived. The Pantasmas knew every rock there was to be found, every bend of a branch. The forest was theirs, and they knew it like they knew each other.

"Alick?" Karter hissed suddenly, pulling her behind a bush.

"What?" Alick hissed back.

"Listen."

Alick closed her eyes and focused on the sounds of the forest. She heard birds chirping, leaves rustling, the wind as it blew, but nothing out of the ordinary.

"What am I listening for?" Alick asked seconds before a loud thwack echoed through the trees. Alick froze. After a while, the thwack sounded again.

"It almost sounds like an ax," Karter whispered.

Alick nodded. It did sound like an ax. But what would an ax be doing in the Rebel Forest? And why here? Alick estimated they were nearly a hundred feet from the nearest path, but the thwacks sounded barely twenty feet off.

Slowly, Alick raised herself off the ground so that she could see over the bush. In the distance Alick could make out a figure, indeed with an ax, chopping away at a large tree. "What is he doing?" Alick muttered out loud, shifting slightly to get a better view.

The tree finally reached its breaking point and fell, right toward Alick and Karter.

"Alick!" Karter gasped, grabbing Alick's waist and pulling her backwards on top of him just as the tree came crashing down, a particularly large branch landing right where Alick had been.

Alick's heart was beating practically out of her chest, both from the near miss and from suddenly finding herself in Karter's arms. She gently extracted herself, putting her finger to her lips and quietly whispering, "shh," as she tried to see where the woodcutter was. Peering over the bush, she caught sight of at least twenty of Fallon's men coming right for them.

Alick sat back down quickly, not realizing she was hyperventilating until Karter asked her what was wrong, what had she seen.

"We have to get out of here," Alick mouthed.

"Where?" Karter asked.

They could both hear the footsteps now, drawing closer. And the voices.

"You sure we shouldn't cut it into pieces first?" one guy said.

"It'll take too long. They need the wood now," said another.

"Well, they need it cut anyway, I don't see why we can't just do it now," the first guy muttered.

Alick's mind was racing, they could not be seen. Not now, not after everything, not when they finally had a chance. They needed to distract the men. Just long enough to move up a tree or behind a larger bush. Just long enough to hide.

Alick looked around for something, anything she could throw. As she began frantically swiveling her head back and forth, Karter laid his hand on her arm.

"What do you need?" he mouthed.

"A distraction," Alick mouthed back.

Alick watched as Karter nodded and picked up a rock she hadn't noticed. He tested its weight in his hand a couple times and then threw it with all his might over the bush. Alick just prayed no one had seen where it had come from.

Luck was with them. Apparently the rock hit one of the men on the head, knocking him to the ground. In the subsequent mayhem, Alick and Karter were able to escape unseen, sneaking low to the ground, deeper into the forest, headed for a point below the Pantasma camp along a route they hoped was clear of any more of Fallon's men. At any rate, now they were on guard. They wouldn't be surprised again. The woods were a dangerous place to be.

CHAPTER 30

"You're back!"

As soon as Karter and Alick set foot inside the clearing where the camp was when they left, the cry went up. Karter and Alick were back. They were safe, and they were back. Within moments, the message had passed through the outer patrol to the inner patrol and into the command tent where Sam and Rydly were.

"Well, well, well, we were beginning to think you'd gotten lost," Peter said, jumping down from a tree across the clearing.

"Where's the camp, Peter?" Alick asked immediately. Karter was wondering that himself. He noticed Peter's swagger was greatly increased and wondered why he'd grown so much more confident. He shifted uncomfortably as Peter walked over. Between falling into the dragon nest, being almost dashed to pieces, and flying all day and night his back was stiff and sore and desperately in need of new bandages.

"Sam and Rydly made the call. We moved the camp deeper into the forest. Fallon's men were drawing too close."

"Too close to here?" Alick turned to Karter, worry etched all over her face.

Peter nodded.

"But if they go through here that trajectory leads them right through the Great Tree!"

"So? It's just a tree, Alick," Peter came over and took her sack. "Now come on, it's not safe here."

Karter grabbed Peter's arm. "You don't understand, Peter."

"And since when do you?" Peter asked with a slight sneer. "Go on an adventure with Alick and suddenly you're the boss?"

Karter had to restrain himself from punching Peter in the face right then and there. He probably would have anyway had Alick not intervened.

"Karter's right, Peter. That tree is more than just wood. It's a spiritual place, almost like a pilgrimage sight. It's a part of this kingdom as much as Heritor Day. You do not mess with that tree."

"Those are old wives tales, Alick. Surely you don't think *Fallon* believes them."

"You'd be surprised how superstitious he is," Alick murmured so quietly only Peter and Karter could hear her.

Karter narrowed his eyes slightly at Peter and then walked past him, following the soldiers leading the way to the new camp. He didn't know when he'd started considering the fighting Pantasmas as soldiers. Most of them were still too young for facial hair. In any decent world, they would barely know how to hold their weapons. To call them anything else, however, wouldn't be fair to them.

The new campsite wasn't that far from the previous one, maybe two hundred feet difference. As Karter walked toward it, he immediately saw the differences from the previous camps. The new campsite was entirely ringed with Pantasmas and large pointed sticks. This was no longer a refugee camp. It was a war camp.

"Alick!" Sam appeared from nowhere and flung her arms around her friend. Karter smiled and kept walking.

"Glad you're back, man," Rydly fell into step with Karter and patted him on the back.

"It's good to be back. I was tired of being attacked by creatures I didn't recognize," Karter said wryly.

"How bad are your injuries?"

"The usual. Cuts, scrapes, bruises. I've got a large gash along my spine that needs attention, and Alick's ankle is sprained, nothing life threatening."

"Did you guys succeed?" Rydly lowered his voice so no one could hear.

Karter nodded, scanning the camp to look inconspicuous. It seemed emptier than usual; the youngest children were sitting around the fire circle playing a game with Tara and Kara, and the older kids were doing their chores.

"Where is everyone?" Karter asked. Anyone over the age of ten seemed to be missing from the usual company with a couple exceptions, all girls.

"Patrol," Rydly said as they entered the command tent. "We have every able-bodied Pantasma out getting experience. We're going to need every single one for the battle so they're in training."

"What about the older girls left at camp? Do they not count?"

"All of those girls are trained. Tara and Kara stopped fighting years ago for personal reasons.

The other older girls in camp are on a rotation basis."

"Why are they still in camp at all?" Karter asked.

"Someone has to keep the children in line. You know how Sam is with them and the boys can barely take care of themselves."

Karter laughed. He couldn't imagine Sam taking care of the children; she was too impatient.

"All right, boys, let's get down to business," Alick said, coming into the tent dramatically.

"We just got back," Karter replied.

"Yes, and we need to get a move on with this whole kingdom siege. We're the smaller group, plus, we're attacking. It's the worst combination. We're going to need a whole lot of planning."

"Should we get Peter if we're strategizing?" Sam asked.

"Nah, I'm sure he'll show up anyway," Alick replied.

Karter snorted his water and nearly started choking, causing Alick to shoot him an amused look.

"You okay?" Rydly asked when Karter could finally breathe again.

"What? Yeah, I'm fine." Karter felt his cheeks burning from embarrassment as he mopped up the water he'd spit. He hadn't meant to spew water everywhere, but sometimes Alick used such a dry, sarcastic, tone, he couldn't help but crack up—it was hilarious.

"So, what's the plan?" Karter asked, joining Alick, Sam, and Rydly in looking at a map of the forest.

"Fallon's men really are pushing deep into the forest," Alick murmured, tracing the routes with her finger.

"We think Fallon's new plan is to build the wall around the Great Tree, to include it within the kingdom."

Karter nodded. "That makes much more sense if he's as superstitious as Alick says."

Sam and Rydly turned together and gave Karter the exact same incredulous look. Then they looked at Alick, who gave a small shake of her head. Karter narrowed his eyes. What had just happened? What had Sam and Rydly asked Alick with their looks that she had answered no too?

"What?" Karter demanded.

"Nothing," Alick said quickly. One of these days he'd crack their secret wordless communication system, but for now he'd have to deal with being in the dark. Karter pursed his lips and looked back down at the map.

"So the dark ones are Fallon's troops?" Karter clarified.

"Yeah, and the white ones are ours," Sam responded, moving a couple markers around.

"That's gotta be at least five to one," Karter exclaimed, examining the pieces.

"Fifteen to one, actually. Each marker is two people," Rydly put in.

"Fifteen to one," Alick gasped, sliding down into a chair. "Fifteen to one." She kept repeating it over and over again.

"Hey, Alick, listen to me." Karter knelt down beside her. "They're just numbers. Just numbers. We'll be fine. We'll determine a wicked strategy and we'll dispose of Fallon the way he deserves. It'll be fine. Don't forget our secret weapon."

Alick looked up into his eyes and nodded.

"Just a number," she repeated, standing back up. "Just a number," she whispered, repeating it to herself again and again.

Karter stood back up as well, but inside he was reeling. 1,500 trained soldiers against 100 raggedy children and two dragons were not great odds. Maybe if they were defending a keep, it would be possible. But 100 attacking a stronghold made to withstand thousands? Even with the dragons and an excellent strategy yet to be determined. How could they ever win? Perhaps Alick was right to despair.

He quietly left the tent. He needed to get new bandages before his back got infected. If he was going to die this year, it would be in battle, not from bacteria.

CHAPTER 31

Alick leaned over the various maps, searching for a tunnel she knew existed. It was the same one she had used to escape all those years ago.

"Ugh!" she exclaimed, tossing aside yet another blueprint. "One of these schematics has got to be helpful!" Alick leaned back down over another blueprint, running her finger along lines she had long since memorized.

"Do you remember exactly where it was, Alick?" Rydly asked, poring over another blueprint. Alick was whipping through the maps and blueprints faster than any of her three mates. She knew the castle layout and surrounding land by heart after all this time, having lived there and studied the maps since she was a girl.

"Somewhere on the ground floor in the servants keep. I remember laundry and a kitchen. I hid in a cupboard for a while." As Alick spoke, she saw flashes of the memory in her mind. It was strange, some parts of the night were so clear in her head. Dinner, when Fallon had made a toast to his soon-to-be bride. Bedtime, the last time she'd seen her parents alive. The flash of the blade as Fallon swept it down through her father as he lay on his bed. The screams of her mother as the same was done to her.

After that, all Alick could remember was the fear. And running. Bits and pieces of the castle as she fled, she remembered the tunnel door and the wet of the moat. She remembered stumbling out into the night in the woods, looking back one last time. She remembered tripping, letting go of her Crista Real, and not bothering to pick it up again.

"Alick?" Karter broke Alick's reverie.

"Yeah?" she asked, taking a deep breath to calm her racing heart.

"Is this it?" Karter pointed to a spot on the map, and Alick nearly tripped over her own feet trying to get over to him to look.

Right under Karter's finger was the small indication of a door, a short rectangle, and another door right above the moat.

"Yes, that's it, Karter!" Alick exclaimed happily, giving him a hug.

"Why exactly have we spent most of the day looking for that?" Sam asked, looking over Karter's other shoulder.

"It's an infiltration route, one of many we're going to have to pinpoint if we want to succeed."

"Why infiltration routes?" Peter asked, coming into the tent.

"For the last time, Peter," Alick snapped. "If you want to be a part of the strategic meetings, just walk in! Stop spying on us."

"All right," Peter replied. "Don't get fussy about it."

Alick opened her mouth to say something sarcastic back, but a small flick from Sam reminded her it was often better to let Peter think he was the boss of them all. It made it easier to undermine him. She let out a frustrated sigh, composed herself, and answered Peter's questions.

"Infiltration routes, because to destroy their advantage of the stronghold, we have to get into the stronghold. The walls are twenty feet high all around, easily manned, and near impossible to scale with such a small army. If we tried to climb, they'd pick us off one by one."

"So we're sneaking in?" Peter asked.

Alick nodded, pointing out the three points of entry they'd located so far: the tunnel, the trash chute, and a drainage culvert. "We'll need a distraction team, a group of people who can put up a fight that looks like it will need all hands on deck, so to speak."

"We'll draw them away from the small entrances, sneak inside, and then the real fighting starts," Karter finished.

"All we need to do is create a truly noteworthy distraction," Alick muttered.

"To draw all of their manpower, we'll need to make them think we outnumber them. We must appear to pose a great threat," Sam said.

Alick smiled widely. "We don't need anything we don't already have," she said, practically laughing.

"No offense, but I doubt one hundred Pantasmas is going to do the trick," Peter grumbled.

Alick shook her head. "Of course not, but twenty-five Pantasmas, two dragons, and some cleverly used scarecrows just might."

"Dragons?" Peter exclaimed.

"Oh yeah, we haven't told you about that yet," Karter said absentmindedly as he drew marks in the table with his knife.

Alick rolled her eyes and confiscated the knife while explaining to Peter about finding the two dragons, leaving out as much detail as she possibly could. Once he believed her—which took a while—even Peter had to admit that having two fire breathing creatures larger than houses would come in handy. The five of them sat around the table and began making in depth plans to cover any and everything that could go wrong.

For the next three days, they sat around the command table and planned. They all knew that if any small detail was left unattended, they would all die. Even with their plan, they'd probably all die; but Alick felt good about their odds. She refused to think of everything that might go wrong, seeing it only abstractly in her head. Laying siege to the castle almost sounded easy on paper: get in, kill Fallon, announce victory. Objectively, they would be fine. Alick refused to let herself think otherwise. Her father had always said, "If you believe in something hard enough, and it's within the realm of normal physics, anything can happen."

They could win this war. Alick believed it with all her heart. She couldn't bring her parents back, but she could make them proud.

It took another two weeks for their plan to be ready for implementation. The scarecrows had to be made and provided with clothing, torches had to be made, weapons found and shined, entry points checked out and verified. But at long last, the Pantasmas were ready. As soon as night fell the next day, they would begin.

The eve of a battle is always tense, everybody wonders what will go wrong, what might go right, the risks, the chances. The stress is paramount, above anything ever felt before. Alick couldn't stand it. She stalked out of the tent and sat near the fire, picking absentmindedly at the guitar-like instrument they had. Before long, others had joined her, banging on logs, strumming other similar instruments, whistling, singing. They were trying to lose themselves in the music, to forget what lay ahead. They were on the brink of something that would change everything. The next day would never be the same as the one before it, but for them the next day could literally change their lives. Or end them.

As the music swelled, the dancing began. Little jigs, folk dances, just to get the body moving, to get the mind to cease swirling. Something to concentrate on. When Karter pulled Alick up to her feet and led her to dance with the rest of the Pantasmas, she didn't even protest. Distractions were good. And this could very well be the last time they could ever dance. The manic charade lasted till dawn, the music swirling, the dancers whirling through the torch-lit night until the first rays of the sun pierced the sky.

Sleep took them, and when they awoke, it was time.

The twenty children who were too young to fight were rounded up and taken to the Great Tree, one by one they were lifted into the branches where they could be the safest. Tara and Kara were armed and positioned at the base of the tree with a horn to blow for reinforcements should their position become compromised.

"Don't hesitate to call if you're found," Alick whispered to Tara as she left the clearing. "These kids are the future, and we need to keep them safe above all else."

Tara nodded, and Alick disappeared through the trees, the next stage of the plan already in motion.

"Alick, wait!" A small voice stopped Alick, and she whipped around.

"Piper!" Alick exclaimed as she recognized the small girl running toward her. "What are you doing here?"

The night was still and quiet as Piper buried her head into Alick's embrace.

"I want to come with you, Alick," Piper whispered.

"Piper, it's too dangerous."

"But what if you don't come back?"

Alick felt her heart clench, and she had to blink rapidly to keep the tears back.

"Listen to me, Piper. I need you to do a very important job for me." Alick took her hand and began leading her back to the tree.

"What is it?" the little girl asked.

"I need you to stay safe. Absolutely safe."

Piper stuck her bottom lip out and pouted. "But that's not what you do."

"But it's what I need *you* to do. You know why?"

"Why?"

Alick knelt down so that she was eye to eye with the little Pantasma. "I need you to stay safe so that if I don't come back, you can make sure that people remember me. Can you do that? Can you make sure that no matter what happens, everyone will know that someone cared for them, someone will always care for them, and that someday, somehow things will look up? Can you do that for me?"

Piper nodded. "No one could ever forget you, Alick, any of you," she whispered. She gave Alick one last hug and scampered back up into the treeline. Alick could only pray that the children would be all right as she ran back the way she came. It was time to meet the dragons.

Deep in the forest, the two beasts waited with the entirety of the Pantasma's force, silent as the grave, just as she'd asked. They were farther to the right in the woods than they'd ever been before in an effort to stay clear of Fallon's men working on the wall. Scouts had reported that Fallon kept his palace armed at all times with at least a thousand men. The other five hundred or so kept track of the workers on the wall. If the work men were forced to join in the fight, it would increase Fallon's force dramatically, so Alick simply prayed that they would take her side, especially if it seemed like she was winning.

Alick arrived at the rendezvous point precisely on schedule where the blue dragon was ready for take off and the red dragon prepared to pull along the scarecrow army. Alick climbed onto her dragon's back and faced the gathered army.

"It is time," she began. "It is time to give Fallon a taste of his own medicine. We may be small in numbers, but we are fierce in might. All of our lives, Fallon has underestimated our power and strength. No longer. By the time the dawn rises, this will be over. For better or for worse, it will be over. The objective is to dispatch Fallon. As soon as he is dead, the battle stops. According to the rules of battle placed down by the witch of Sombas, the chosen heir from Heritor Day is the rightful ruler the minute the old ruler's heart stops beating.

"It will be a long, arduous night, but let's fight for what we're worth. Fight for every person Fallon has taken from us—parents, brothers, sisters, companions in arms. Fight with sword and knife, tooth and claw. Ladies and gentlemen, let's give them something to remember us by."

Alick turned and took off into the air, the cheers of the Pantasmas quickly fading behind her as she soared up into the night. When she could see the castle, she signaled her dragon, and a burst of fire lit up the night sky. Down below, the distraction force began to move forward while the three infiltration groups spread out to go around the castle. The siege of Conquistado had begun.

CHAPTER 32

Moonlight lit the paths as Karter led his men on through the dark. The only sound was the dull thumps of the dragons feet, which drowned out the feet of the Pantasmas. Above, Alick flew silently in circles on her dragon, waiting for them to catch up. A dragon walking was much slower then a dragon flying, but that was okay. Karter needed to give the infiltration teams time to make it to the castle, plus, it would be difficult to get the fake army to the castle without a dragon pulling them along. They were quite heavy and difficult to manage.

Karter glanced back at the rolling scarecrows; there had to be hundreds of them, all situated in perfect battle formation, wearing the garb of the Pantasmas and holding lit torches high above their straw heads. In the dark, they looked just like the archers that walked behind them. Once they made it to the front gates of the castle, the archers would sneak onto the rolling platform and take the places of missing scarecrows, ready to shoot arrows and extend the illusion of a large army.

Around the next bend, the castle came into sight. The village lay to both sides, the villagers' peeping eyes were just visible in the windows. Karter saluted them, praying they would stay in their homes where they would be safe.

This was the Pantasmas' fight. The small band of thieves had been protecting the people from afar for a decade. Now they would give one last fight. Tonight, it would end.

In the sky, Alick's dragon let out another burst of fire, straight up like an arrow. The infiltration groups would know that Karter had been spotted by the castle guards. He took a deep breath and focused on the castle as light after light turned on. The entire palace was in an uproar, and his task force was the cause.

"Your move, Fallon," he whispered.

As he came to a halt in front of the gates, Karter was awestruck at the power he possessed. The dragon, who he had decided to name Ameazante, was large enough that Karter could just see over the wall to the castle beyond. It was gorgeous. And up in the arches, above the stained glass windows, was Alick's Crista Real, mosaicked where all could see.

"Look at that, proof we're doing the right thing," Karter muttered to his dragon.

Karter put that image and its implications to the back of his mind; it could wait.

The outer wall was swarming with guards and they all had arrows aimed right at his head.

"Alick, now would be a really good time to fly back down," Karter whispered under his breath, looking up into the starry sky where Alick hovered on her dragon.

As if she could hear him, her dragon let out one final blast of fire, right toward the center of the grounds, between the outer wall and the castle, igniting the grass as Alick dropped down right next to Karter.

"You ready for this?" Karter asked.

Alick shook her head. "Not in the slightest." She stood up onto her dragon's head and pulled out her sword, standing there, looking every bit like the Queen she should be. The fire in the grounds spread quickly, the grass being dry and brittle just as Alick had suspected. It drew the attention they needed.

"Here in Conquistado, under the moonlight and stars, I, Alick Karenza Daveney, challenge Derex Fallon, King, to a battle for the crown. When your heart beats its last, I shall rule this land as it was meant to be ruled—as Libre! By the edicts of Heritor Day, I invoke the challenge I am allowed here and now!"

Karter held his breath. The battle hung before them like the last thread holding together an intricate tapestry. Cut the thread and all was lost. All they had to do was wait for Fallon to bring forth his scissors.

Up on the walk, a man appeared. Karter recognized him as the priest from Heritor Day, except now instead of his stately robes the poor man was in nothing but his dressing gown, pulled tight against his frail body.

"Derex Fallon recognizes your challenge and invites the fight." The old man's voice wavered before he went on. "His troops are mobilized and ready. However, before you throw your lives away, he has asked his chief general to offer terms of surrender. Please welcome Martino Masashi, Commander of Arms of Conquistado."

Karter rolled his eyes. The amount of formality involved with the siege was ridiculous. What happened to the days when you could just attack? At least this gave Karter and Alick time to judge how many soldiers were focused on them, and it gave the infiltration teams time to get into place.

Martino Marsashi, a short man with a bit of mustache and a fierce expression, appeared on the battlements dressed, unlike the priest, in his full uniform complete with more medals than Karter felt like counting. "You have five minutes to surrender with your pathetic army of still torch bearers, or we shall attack you without mercy. None will leave here alive."

Karter looked over at Alick, whose gaze had gone stony and determined.

"We shall not run like abashed dogs, Marsashi. And our torch bearers, as you call them, are perfectly competent.

"Ready! Aim!—"

"You shoot and we shall not forgive," Marsashi screamed, his accent sharp and foreign.

"Fire!" Alick screamed, and twenty-five arrows whizzed over Karter's and Alick's heads, each one finding a target on the battlements. The battle for Libre had begun. It was time to draw their fire.

CHAPTER 33

Dragon fire blazed in the night, and screams rent the air as Alick and Karter drew Fallon's troops to the front of the castle. Within moments of the commencement of the battle, Alick's dragon leapt into the air and let out three distinct blasts, the signal to the infiltration groups. But only half of Fallon's troops were present at the distraction point.

"Let's go," Alick yelled to Karter, who had risen up in the air behind her.

Together they flew over the castle, burning the grass and trees, landing on the castle wall, and giving chase to runaway soldiers, drawing the eyes and fire of almost all of Fallon's forces as they scorched rows of men at a time. *If only the walls weren't so sturdily built*, Alick thought to herself as her dragon landed on yet another section of wall, squishing a catapult and leaving large dragon footprints on the stone battlements, but leaving the wall intact. Her dragon breathed fire again, crisping the entire section of wall.

Alick had been smart not to assume the dragons could breach the wall for her troops—they barely left dents. Alick took off again and landed on the back of the castle where unsuspecting troops whipped around and looked at her with wild eyes. Alick could only imagine how she looked, riding upon a dragon in the fiery night. It was probably like something out of a fairy tale.

"What are you doing back here, boys?" she asked wryly. "Don't you know the fighting's at the other end of the castle?" Alick heard Karter land behind her.

"Now!" Alick shouted, and together, the two dragons shot twin blasts of flame along the battlements, sending the troops running along the walls toward the distraction point, the dragons chasing them along the wall. Alick grabbed her bow from her back and began shooting at the running masses, trying to increase disorder and panic. No one could be paying attention to the ground. They had to focus on the sky.

They were well-trained soldiers, as soon as they could get organized, the distraction team was toast. They would figure out the mass of scarecrows was just that. Alick and Karter's only hope at this point was to try and cause as much chaos as they could, keep them unorganized.

The first couple rows of scarecrows were ablaze from a catapult, and many of the straw men had fallen over from the arrows raining at them above. But the twenty-five archers among the scarecrows were doing an excellent job keeping up the illusion and near as Alick could tell, the Pantasmas among the group were relatively unharmed. The scarecrows acted like shields from arrows, and the fire kept Fallon's men from coming in with swords.

More screams rent the air, and Alick caught sight of Karter's dragon eating several soldiers it had caught trying to jump off the wall. To her dismay, Alick also noticed that the soldiers were organizing, forming a triangle, with troops facing either dragon and the distraction team by the gates. They were mobilizing.

Alick kicked her dragon into the air, flying high above the castle, away from the quickly recuperating army. The element of surprise was gone for the moment. She watched as the twenty-five archers scrambled away from the scarecrow platforms as they were fired upon continuously with catapults. It wouldn't be long now before their ruse was discovered.

"Come on, Sam," Alick muttered before dodging a flaming rock. Alick had her dragon shoot a blast of flame in the direction it had come from, hopefully destroying the catapult responsible.

The beat of wings brought Alick's attention back to reality as Karter pulled up alongside her.

"What's taking them so long?" he called across the air.

Alick threw her hands in the air. "How should I know, but they had better hurry up!" The two dragons flew apart as a cloud of arrows threatened to envelope them. The army was fully mobilized now, yet the infiltration groups hadn't sent the signal.

As Alick was about to lose hope, the expected explosion sent rock and debris flying high through the air as the smallest tower blew apart. It was the least used of all the towers, and as it flew into pieces, Alick could only pray that the infiltration teams had done their duty and evacuated the tower of innocents before the blast. Now was not the time to worry about that, though. The blast had drawn the attention of the soldiers. They knew they'd been duped. From every tower window, a Pantasma flag hung down. The castle was taken, and the advantage was now theirs.

Alick smiled in spite of herself. The infiltration teams had done their job. They'd snuck into the castle, rigged the explosive, secured the exits, and were ready to battle Fallon's forces, which were now forced to re-conquer their own territory before Alick could get to the King, or Alick won.

Alick caught Karter's eye, and together, they flew over the burning grounds to the castle, scrambling off of the flying dragons onto the large balcony that ran the length of the front of the building. Alick touched the columns fondly— she was home. The two scrambled to the nearest door, got their swords out, and entered the castle. It was time to end this.

CHAPTER 34

Candelabras lined the hallway, casting a warm rosy glow down the stone corridor. Karter stopped looking up and down the hallway at the tapestries that hung resolutely down, at the suits of armor decorating the specially carved niches. If it wasn't for the screams outside, you would never know there was a war going on. Karter glanced behind him at Alick, but Alick wasn't there anymore. Karter spun in a circle but didn't see Alick anywhere.

"Alick?" he hissed, his sword held out, ready for attack.

"Over here." Alick's voice carried, and Karter was able to locate her crawling in the shadows by a niche directly opposite a magnificent tapestry that featured a young maiden standing alone on a rock in the middle of the sea as a storm rolled in. Karter hoped it wasn't prophetic.

"What are we doing?" Karter asked, kneeling down next to Alick.

"Looking for the trigger," Alick muttered, running her hands along the back of the suit of armor.

"The what?" Karter asked. He looked around the hallway again, making sure that they were really alone. He didn't want any stray soldiers still in the castle sneaking up on him.

"It's around here somewhere." Alick's voice was barely audible.

Suddenly, there was a loud click and the tapestry behind them rolled up with a snap.

Karter's mouth dropped open as he surveyed the tunnel that had appeared.

"Alick, what's that?"

"A tunnel."

"I got that part. Why is it there?"

"Every castle has secret passages."

"Yes, but they're generally secret," Karter grumbled as he followed Alick into the narrow passageway. He was expecting cobwebs and spiders, the usual signs of disuse one would expect to find in an abandoned tunnel, but their was nothing. There wasn't even any dust. "Alick, there's something wrong. Why is this passage so well used?"

Alick shushed him and pulled him down a side passage where there were no lights shortly before several maids ran by in the main corridor. Down and down they went until they came to a small ladder cut into the side of the wall.

"Up you go," Alick said.

"Alick, what's going on?"

"I'll tell you when you get up there; it's not safe."

Karter pursed his lips and began to climb up into the ceiling. The next room was dusty, making Karter feel a tiny bit better, because it meant they were more likely to remain undiscovered for the time being. He glanced about the tiny room and nearly jumped out of his skin when he spotted two other people already sitting on crates.

"Shh!" Rydly motioned.

Karter nodded, his heart racing at two miles a minute. He hadn't realized the rendezvous point was so obscure.

Alick popped up out of the floor and slid the panel shut behind her.

"All right, guys, we're in."

Karter didn't like the look of the evil glint in her eye as she sat down in the dust. It usually meant she had a very dangerous plan up her sleeve.

"Can someone please explain to me where we are?" Karter began.

"We're in the servant's passages," Alick answered. "They're used by the staff to easily navigate the castle. They run to every room."

"How did you know how to get in?" Karter asked incredulously.

"Karter, I lived here for years." Alick gave him a strange look. "Did you never go exploring as a kid?"

"No, actually. I got in trouble whenever I did."

Alick and Sam both laughed at that.

"Clearly, you weren't very good at sneaking," Alick said with a smile. Karter had to agree with that, as a child he could never get away with anything. He was too honest, and he was often betrayed by his brother.

"Status update?" Alick interrupted Karter's memories.

"My group got in fine. We surprised a lot of the servants, but a few threats kept them quiet as we moved out. I think a lot of them were actually on our side," Sam started. Her infiltration group had gone in through the trash chute, right into the kitchens.

"My group hit a small rough spot: a few young guards on their way to the battle. We knocked them out and tied them up before they could cause any harm." Rydly had gone in through the tunnel, which apparently came up in the pantry, adjacent to the kitchen.

"Any news from Peter?" Alick asked.

"None. But the explosion went as planned, which means he managed to get the bomb in place and press his third of the detonator control," Sam reasoned.

"I'm sure he's fine, Alick," Karter tried to reassure her, noticing her rather pensive expression.

Karter took a deep breath. "All right, so let's take stock. We're all in the castle, trying to keep Fallon's forces out. We've blown up a tower, hopefully while no one was in it. We're in a small, unused storage room in the servants' passages, and we need to get to Fallon. Did I miss anything?"

The other three shook their heads.

"All righty, then," Karter continued. "How do we find Fallon?"

"Sam and I should go find our troops again. We need to stay organized if we want to continue holding the castle," Rydly said.

"That's actually smart, Riddle," Sam muttered.

Karter watched as Rydly opened his mouth to retort something rude back, but Alick shushed them all and scampered over to the corner where she started moving boxes.

"Alick, what are you doing?" Sam asked.

"Shh! And help me," Alick hissed, frantically shoving at the crates. Karter stood up to help, easily sliding the various boxes aside, revealing a small round hole in the floor that looked straight down through a light fixture into the kitchen. If Karter listened carefully, he could just make out the conversation of the kitchen workers below.

"The kids are in every room of the castle, blockading every door and shooting arrows from all the windows," one voice said.

"How could they possibly have accumulated so much power? Fallon couldn't even wage war like that," another voice answered.

"They don't really, there's only one or two kids a room. If Fallon's troops come back through, it'll be a slaughter," a third voice put in gravely. "Though lots of the younger staff that Fallon stripped from their families have gone to help."

"Lord help us," the first voice said. "There'll be no children left."

"Maybe they'll prevail?" the second voice ventured.

"What have you been drinking?" the third voice cut in harshly. "The girl is nowhere to be found. She'll never take Fallon's life."

"I don't know, she's been wreaking havoc for years," a fourth voice spoke up, this one was younger, almost child-like. "Everyone looks up to her."

"And yet Fallon has never really tried to do anything about her and her groupies," the third voice pointed out. "If he doesn't think she's a threat, she can't possibly be."

"Maybe he's underestimating her," the fourth voice insisted. "You know how little he thinks of us women. Thinks we're useless."

The voices began to fade as they moved toward another end of the room below.

"Come back," Alick breathed. "Tell us where he is. Tell us where to find Fallon." But the voices were gone.

"That was the most unhelpful overheard conversation I've ever listened to," Karter grumbled.

Alick whacked him on his arm. "Not helping."

Karter blushed. He hadn't meant to annoy Alick.

"What's our plan?" he asked.

Rydly and Sam were sitting on a pair of boxes back toward the front of the room again, right above the trapdoor, and Alick was moving to join them as she answered, "Sam and Rydly can go help the troops. Keep Fallon's men out. You and I will continue through the passages, listening for word on where Fallon is. Eventually we'll either find him, or he'll find us."

"Let's hope for the first," Sam said ominously.

"Do you have to be such a downer?" Rydly snapped.

"Rydly—" Alick started, but she never got the chance to cut the argument. Rydly had lost it.

"Everyday, all the time, you're always putting everyone down. I'm sick of it. Here we are, cramped in a cupboard, examining our imminent deaths, and all you can do is offer half-hearted well wishes that all will go well." On and on Rydly went.

Karter could only watch in amazement as his friend finally let out every emotion he'd been harboring against Sam in one go, turning beet red and then purple. Beside him, Karter could tell Alick was equally astonished, though one look at her face told him she was also horrified.

Karter didn't blame her. Rydly painted a much more horrific image of Sam than he'd come to associate with the girl. Yes, she could be harsh, but it was all an act. She wasn't like Alick, who could somehow command the attention of everyone simply by standing up. She would be completely ignored, just another pretty face, if she hadn't made everyone completely scared of her. Her entire attitude was just a front, probably gained while she was on her own in the woods. After all, she'd been a refugee longer than even Alick.

Occasionally in his rant, Rydly would hit upon an actual defect in Sam's personality, but everyone had defects. Alick could be insecure, Karter often doubted himself and those around him, and Rydly was a pushover. Or at least he *had* been a pushover. Karter had a feeling something in Rydly had finally snapped. He would still be Rydly, the Rydly that Alick knew and had grown up with, but now he'd have a backbone. Karter smirked in spite of himself. Rydly with a backbone would be as dangerous as giving Sam a cutlass and calling her Samantha. Both would render the user effectively unstoppable, the perfect match for this war. If they could get him to shut up and focus, that is.

CHAPTER 35

Words are dangerous weapons, in some ways more so than swords. Alick had always thought this to be true, but as she watched Rydly finally snap, she *knew* it to be true. For years, she had watched Sam pile harsh words on him, warning her someday he would get her back.

Every time Sam had brushed her off, saying he was weak, that he was too afraid of Alick to ever try a revenge tactic, but Sam had never understood what Alick meant. Alick knew Rydly wasn't the kind of person to ever get back by physical means. She knew that when he'd finally had enough of Sam, the fallout would be verbal. And she was right. But now was not the time.

As Rydly raged on, Alick looked at Sam and saw a single tear fall down her face. Alick couldn't help but feel sorry for her friend. Though the admonishment was long deserved for her treatment of Rydly, not all the words were. Some of them were so harsh Alick couldn't help but gasp and reprimand Rydly. Not that he was listening, of course. Finally, Rydly stopped and Alick jumped up quickly before Sam could even think of retaliating.

"All right, now is *not* the time for this. Rydly, Sam was just being truthful; she wasn't trying to be a downer; she was trying to show us the reality with which we are faced. Can I trust you two to work together to make this siege a success?" Alick held her breath and looked to Karter for backup. Karter held his hands up and backed up a bit.

Alick rolled her eyes, but she got the message. Karter wasn't going to interfere. It wasn't his mess to get involved in. It wasn't really Alick's either, but Rydly and Sam were her two best friends. She hated it when they fought, and they had bigger fish to fry right now. The clock was ticking. Finally, Sam addressed Rydly.

"Do you feel better?" she asked, only slightly sarcastically.

Rydly straightened his sword and looked her right in the eye. "Not really, actually. We're still all going to die."

"Now who's being the downer?" Sam countered.

Alick opened her mouth to try and mediate, but Sam stopped her. "Alick, one of these days we've got to find peace on our own. It might as well be today."

"You have five minutes max. We've got a war to win." Alick crossed her arms and sat down next to Karter, seething. They couldn't afford the delay, but the Pantasmas would never win if their generals were arguing. It was a rock and a hard place.

"You know, we could leave them," Karter whispered.

"No, they might draw weapons!" Alick whispered back. In front of them, Sam and Rydly had their eyes locked, still fighting about who was more cross.

They kept their voices level, a blessing considering they were hiding in enemy turf, but each word was packed with so much emotion, Alick was surprised neither Sam nor Rydly was bleeding from the sharpness.

"Rydly, we have to go get the troops," Sam was saying, trying to reason with the beast. *Ironic actually*, Alick thought.

"No, I will win this argument."

"What argument is there to win? You're yelling and I'm accepting that. Move on."

"Why must you alway knock me down?"

"Everyone needs to be knocked down occasionally to remind them to get back up again."

"That is the stupidest thing I've ever heard."

"You said it!"

"Rydly said that?" Karter whispered to Alick.

"Yeah, I'm surprised Sam remembers. It was a couple years back. Every time Sam tried to give up teaching the kids how to sword fight, Rydly would push her over," Alick whispered back. She looked over and saw him staring at her incredulously. "What?" she asked.

"Rydly would push Sam over?" Karter clarified.

Alick nodded. "Yeah, it was my idea. Not sure she ever figured that out, though. I think she thought Peter put him up to it."

Karter continued to look at her with amazement, but Alick turned her attention back to the argument just in time to see Sam walk across the room and slap Rydly across the face and yell, "Snap out of it!"

"Sam!" Alick yelped. She jumped up, very confused, and worried someone had heard Sam shout. Everyone was confused by what happened next, though. Rydly narrowed his eyes, touched his face where it was rapidly turning red, and then began to advance on Sam.

"Rydly, she didn't mean it." Alick went to halt him, but Karter grabbed her.

"I don't think he's going to hurt her," Karter said, a touch of wonder in his voice.

Alick struggled against Karter's grip, but it wasn't budging, so she looked back to Sam and Rydly. Sam had backed up, but when her foot hit a crate she stopped, looking nervous for the first time in a long while. Meanwhile Rydly kept advancing while worry twisted Alick's stomach into knots.

When Rydly was a foot away from Sam he stopped, looked her straight in the eye, and then closed the gap and kissed her.

Alick felt her jaw drop as she watched Sam, not recoil in horror and slap him again, but actually return the affection, wrapping her arms around Rydly and pulling him closer.

Alick was so stunned, she didn't even realize Karter had let go of her.

"There, see, they're fine," Karter whispered in her ear.

Alick whipped around. "You knew this would happen?" she asked. She still couldn't process what was going on.

Karter nodded. "Well, not exactly, but I suspected they were more fond of each other more than they let on."

"How?" Alick's mind was in overdrive.

"You know I was bullied by my brother my entire life."

"Yes," Alick said.

"Bullies bully everyone, and they don't feel bad about it. When I first met Sam, I thought she was a bully, but as I got to know you and the camp, I realized she wasn't. It's a front. Yes, she's rough around the edges, but she's no bully. She never purposefully hurt Rydly. She might have on occasion accidentally gone too far in her teasing, but she never meant it."

"So?" Alick was still entranced by the scene; it was so out of place, she wondered if she was dreaming.

"So I figured neither of them could figure out how to flirt, so they went for hating each other instead."

"What?" Alick blinked rapidly in confusion.

"Love and hate are very closely intertwined. In some ways, hate is easier. It doesn't break your heart."

"We all hate Fallon and I'm pretty sure that's got nothing to do with love," Alick muttered.

"Would you hate him quite so much if he hadn't taken everything you loved?" Karter whispered.

Alick bit her lip and said, "Enough of this, we've got a war to win. Go get them to stop."

Karter moved over to the couple, placed a hand on each of their shoulders, and gently pried them apart. "As touching as this is, we might very well all be dead by morning," he said simply. "You might want to wait a bit and go find your troops."

"Um...right!" Sam said hastily, scrambling over to the door in the floor. "You coming, Rydly?" she asked, poised to lower herself into the corridor below. Alick caught her eye and smiled. Sam rolled her eyes and blushed in return.

"Don't die. Either of you," Alick pleaded.

"Don't you worry, Alick." Rydly said as he moved toward the ladder, seeming a little stunned himself. "We'll both be around to watch you be crowned Queen, I swear it." Alick felt her heart clench as her two best friends ran off to the front lines.

"Oh, I hope they'll be okay."

"They'll likely be safer than us, Alick," Karter said. "Come on. I don't know the way." Alick took one last look around the safe storeroom and then followed Karter down the ladder. It was time to go into the fire. She shook her head to clear the last few minutes. There would be time to dwell on them later. She was more than used to burying memories.

Alick led the way through the various passages, listening at doors and hiding when voices approached.

"This is taking too long!" Alick vented. Time was difficult to keep track of in the tunnels, but Alick knew an awful lot of it had passed while they tried to find Fallon. She didn't know how much longer her troops could last.

"Let's just go in the next door."

"I don't see how that will help."

"It will let us know where we are."

"I know where we are!"

"So where are we?"

Alick froze. They were in the place she knew best out of the whole castle. The place Fallon *knew* she knew the best. Either he was in that room waiting for her, or something was.

"My bedroom," Alick whispered, her hand on the door.

Behind her, she felt Karter go completely still, realizing the implication in her words.

"Well, worst case scenario is that they catch us and we're dead," he reasoned.

Alick bit her lip and glared at him. "You are such a ray of sunshine sometimes," she growled.

"I was trying to ease the tension," he replied defensively.

"Yeah well, not helping." Alick turned the doorknob and pushed, bursting into the room her sword ready for combat. But the room was empty.

"Well so much for that idea," Karter came in behind her and shut the door.

Alick gave him a look.

"Sorry, doing it again," he apologized. He started walking around the room, running his hand along the paneling that edged her room. Alick could only look around in amazement. Her room looked exactly as it had the night she'd left, right down to the now empty glass of water on the nightstand. Her dolls were all asleep in their beds, her clothes mostly hung neatly in the wardrobe, the door open a crack. The room looked dusty, but not nearly as dusty as it should have been. Someone obviously came in semi-regularly to dust.

"It's like he expected me to come back," Alick murmured to herself.

"Or he just didn't care enough to empty it," Karter murmured back.

Alick blushed. She hadn't realized Karter was listening to her. Alick made her way over to the vanity at the end of the room. Her various hairpins lay strewn across the top; she never did clean them up that night like her mother had asked her too.

On one corner, nestled in its box, was a necklace Alick remembered all too well. It was from her betrothed: the son of a King whose brother would get the throne. He'd given her the necklace for her fifth birthday, a promise of the union in her future. Alick touched the gorgeous silver necklace with the interlaced blue stones. Her mother hadn't ever let her wear it. It was to be a special trinket for her sixteenth birthday, the night she would have been properly engaged to her future husband.

It was strange to think of the life she could have had. Alick closed the necklace box and slipped it into her pocket, a couple hairpins falling in as well.

"We better move on, Karter." Alick turned just in time to see the sword and dodge it. The mirror behind her shattered, spraying Alick's back with glass and cutting the hand of her attacker.

"Stop struggling or we'll kill the boy."

Alick looked up to see a soldier holding Karter with a dagger to his throat.

"Don't listen to them, Alick! Run!" Karter yelled. But it was too late. Someone had already grabbed Alick's wrists. They were caught.

CHAPTER 36

Karter sat in the jail cell banging his head gently against the wall he sat against. They had one job: don't get caught. So much for that. Alick hadn't said a single word since they'd been caught except to ask why they weren't being taken to Fallon. Apparently, Karter and Alick had woken his majesty, who had then decided to take breakfast and would not bother to be interrupted from it. Karter rolled his eyes at the memory. He hoped Alick was plotting. But as he looked over at her dejected figure, he figured it was probably unlikely.

"So what now?" Karter asked. He hadn't realized he'd asked the question aloud until Alick answered him.

"Die, I guess," Alick responded with a sigh. Karter heard her shift her weight and then let out a muffled "ow".

"You okay?" he asked turning to look at her.

"Just sat on something," Alick replied, sticking her hand in her pocket. Karter went back to staring at the ceiling until Alick's michevious laugh echoed around the cell.

"That doesn't sound good," Karter blurted out, sitting upright quickly.

"How about I pick the lock?" Alick said, only slightly manically. She brandished a hairpin and moved to the cell door.

"Have you ever picked a lock before?" Karter asked, allowing hope to blossom in his chest.

"Nope."

Hope gone. Karter slumped back against the side of the cell. He'd read enough books as a child to know that picking locks was an acquired skill. The likelihood of Alick actually managing to open the door was slim indeed. Visions of his family began to fill Karter's mind. His sisters playing hide and seek in the halls, hiding behind tapestries and suits of armor. His parents sitting proudly at the head of the table, happy, if not with him. Karter watched Alick picking at the lock with glazed over eyes, seeing her but mentally being far, far away in his own kingdom, when everything had seemed so simple.

"Alick?" Karter ventured after a while. He wondered what time it was, if the Pantasmas were still holding strong or if they had fallen.

"Yes, Karter?" Alick answered. But Karter could tell she wasn't really focused on him; she was still trying to pick the lock. It was a marvelous thing, perseverance. She'd never be able to tell herself she didn't try.

"There's something I haven't told you."

"If you're only telling me because you think you're going to die. I'd rather you didn't," Alick sighed.

Karter thought about that. "No, I'd probably tell you eventually anyway. Might as well be now."

Alick shrugged. "Shoot then."

Should he really tell her? Karter felt his stomach twisting in knots. When he'd left his kingdom, he had sworn he would never tell anyone who he was. This was the secret he had carried these several months.

"I'm not really who you think I am."

Karter clenched up as the gentle scraping of the hairpin in the lock paused for a second. But Alick started struggling with the lock again shortly after.

"You're not Lynton Karter..." Alick trailed off momentarily. "What *is* your last name?" she asked suddenly, turning to face him.

"Rider," Karter answered. Alick cocked her head to one side. Then she shrugged again and went back to picking the lock. "And yes, that is my name."

"Then I don't really understand where you're going with this." Alick's voice was muffled as she kept her head so close to the bars, Karter would be surprised if she didn't end up with imprints of the design on her forehead.

Karter opened and closed his mouth several times. He just couldn't find the words to tell her.

"Have you ever heard of Outeiro?" Karter finally ventured. The gentle scraping of the pick in the lock was starting to remind him of rats. He would say anything to cover it up.

"Next kingdom over, isn't it?" Alick asked. "To the southeast?"

"Yeah." Karter blinked. He hadn't expected Alick to know that. But then again, she had lived in the castle, her parents were nobility, so she'd probably seen maps. Then again, she might have even visited. Outeiro was always receiving nobles from neighboring realms. Karter mulled this over for a while, trying to recall if he'd ever seen Alick when she was a little girl.

"Is there a point to this conversation?" Alick asked, pulling Karter back to the present.

"Um, yeah..." Karter got up and started pacing. He hadn't realized how difficult this was going to be. "I sort of lied to you when I said I was banished because I was the weaker twin of a noble."

"So what? You were banished because you murdered a guy?" Meanwhile, the gentle scritch-scratch of metal on metal continued putting Karter's nerves on edge.

"No, I was banished because I was the weaker twin."

"Karter, did they hit you on the head?"

"No! Alick, I'm serious!"

"So am I. You aren't making any sense."

"I'm not the son of a noble. I'm the son of the King, Alick. The first born prince of Outeiro, banished for being the sickly child."

"Technically speaking, the King is a noble," Alick replied without missing a beat.

"Well, yes, but..." Karter furrowed his eyebrows and turned to Alick's crouched figure. "What?" he asked, genuinely perplexed. "Did you not hear me?"

"I heard you, Karter. You're a prince."

Karter blinked. Of all the reactions he had prepared himself for upon admitting his secret to

Alick, indifference had not been one of them. He sat down with a thud.

Alick looked over at him. "Are you all right?" she asked, finally putting the pin down.

Karter looked up at her. "Why don't you care?" he asked, studying her. She bit her lip and knelt down in front of him, pulling something out of her pocket.

"Do you recognize this, Karter?" She opened the box, revealing an intricate silver necklace with dark blue gems.

Karter shook his head. It was beautiful, but Karter couldn't recall ever seeing it before.

Alick reached forward and flipped over the largest gem. Karter leaned closer and then gasped. Etched in the silver was his family crest. Karter lifted the necklace from the box and brought it closer to him, studying the detail.

"I don't understand."

"You're not the only one with a secret identity, Karter." Karter lowered the necklace and looked at Alick, whose gaze was locked on his own.

"I've never explicitly told you who my parents were," she whispered.

"They were noble."

"Did you never think it strange, Karter, that a noble family would live in the palace?"

Karter let that sink in. He'd honestly never thought about it much, assuming it was a weird tradition of the kingdom. But Alick was right. Nobles had their own grand homes; they didn't live in the palace proper. He remembered how Alick was a natural leader, how she seemed to know Fallon, how there'd been a tiara in her bedroom. He remembered Rydly avoiding the subject of the late king's child and the way Fallon had purposefully not uttered Alick's last name on Heritor Day.

"Who are you, Alick?" Karter whispered. Alick took his hands, took a deep breath, and looked him straight in the eye.

"My name is Alick Karenza Daveney. I am the daughter of Paxton Alexander and Eowyn Katima Daveney, the late King and Queen of Libre. When I was six years old, my soon to be uncle, William Derex Fallon, led a mutiny, killing my parents and coming after me. I escaped, and he married my aunt, Gabrielle Kana." Alick paused and looked down.

Karter felt his heart slowly breaking as he listened. It was one thing to have your parents murdered. It was quite another to have them murdered by your uncle. Karter reached, extracted one of his hands from Alick's grip, and used it to lift her chin back up.

"I've been running from Fallon my whole life, Karter. He took everything from me when he was a child. He's about to do it again."

Karter shook his head. "I won't let that happen, Alick." He reached forward and hugged her, comforting her. "We're so close, Alick. We can do this." Karter got up and walked over to the jail cell door. If he wasn't mistaken, he could've sworn he'd heard a small click right before Alick had stopped trying to pick the lock to come over to him.

Here goes nothing, Karter prayed and then he pushed open the door.

"Has that been unlocked the whole time?" Alick groaned.

Karter had to smile. "No, you managed to catch the locking mechanism right before you stopped."

"Well, that was luck."

"Always is. Now come on, it's time we took back your kingdom."

CHAPTER 37

Practically paralyzing fear rippled through Alick's body as she and Karter ran along the passageways toward the center parlor. It was the most likely place for Fallon to take his breakfast. Who takes breakfast at 4 in the morning? Alick guessed that was what time it was. The sun wasn't coming up yet, but the sky was definitely lighter than it had been when Alick and Karter first entered the castle.

The center parlor looked out through one of the stained glass windows in the front, right over where Alick guessed the fighting was most likely to be taking place, judging by the sounds and from common sense. The large balcony across the front of the castle was the easiest place to try and force entry as Fallon's forces were trying to do. Fallon wouldn't want to miss the action.

"Turn here, turn here!" Alick cried. She had gotten lost twice already, and she could almost feel the minutes ticking by. Strangely enough, only the continuing sounds of battle kept her sane. If there was still a battle, then there were still Pantasmas. Alick just needed them to hold on a little longer. At long last, Alick found the right door and put her ear up against it. Fallon's chilling voice could be heard on the other side.

Alick sank to the ground, breathing quickly. Fear was quickly taking over. Her heart was racing, and her hands were cold and clammy. Fallon had always frightened her. So had killing. She wasn't sure she had the strength to take a life and live with that guilt.

"Deep breaths, Alick. Don't think about it. It's just another raid. Just another meeting. You have the strength, Alick," Karter whispered in her ear.

Alick nodded. She swallowed and stood up. Fear made her shaky, but it wouldn't stop her. It would never stop her. She slid the door open a crack, glad it was well-oiled and silent. Peeking through the crack, she saw Fallon had his back to her. Four guards ringed the room with another two holding someone by the arms. The prisoner raised his head and Alick gasped. It was Peter.

His face was swollen, his nose and mouth bloody and bruised. But it was definitely Peter.

"I will ask you again," Fallon was saying. "Karenza and the boy have escaped. I want to know how and where to."

"I told you, I don't know, Fallon," Peter spat, earning himself a punch to the gut from one of the soldiers.

"We have to stop them!" Alick hissed to Karter.

"You stay here," he whispered. "I'll go around through the hallway and find a way to distract the guards, get them away so you have a clear shot."

"It's too dangerous, Karter." Alick pulled back from the crack and grabbed his sleeve before he could leave.

"It has to be done," Karter replied, his voice cracking slightly. "Your best chance at this is getting Fallon alone."

Alick shut her eyes. "Go to the end of this hall, there should be a door labelled "hall". Backtrack and catch their attention. Run like the wind. Find the staircase. One floor down is the brunt of the battle. You'll probably be able to lose them, but be careful. Find Sam and Rydly if you can. Make sure they're okay. Make sure they're still safe," Alick felt her voice failing as she contemplated for the first time since saying goodbye to her two friends that she might never see them again. It was too painful.

Suddenly Karter was hugging her, his arms wrapped protectively around her. "I'm sure they're fine. They are the leaders right now. If the battle's still raging, I'm sure they're still kicking away." He pulled back enough to see her eyes, and Alick was suddenly very conscious of their proximity to each other and of Fallon barely a wall away. They were in danger; there was no time for this. But she couldn't ignore the fact that they were mere inches from each other. She could almost feel his heartbeat against hers.

Karter seemed to sense her trail of thought: now wasn't the time, because he leaned back a little more. But, he didn't let go. She could see his eyes dimly in the small light that came through the door, and she could see his body, ready to leave with his eyes refusing to follow.

"Karter," she mouthed, leaning forward slightly, trying to convey all she felt. Together they were safe, they had survived so much together. Karter nodded, pulling back completely.

"I *will* be back, Alick," he whispered. "I promise." And then he was gone, off down the hall to serve as bait.

Alick bit her lip and put her eye back to the crack, waiting for the signal she knew was sure to come. Part of her followed Karter down the hall, tracking his progress, timing his distraction, trying to ignore how close his lips had been, trying to ignore how much she wished he had kissed her, and trying to ignore the fact that they might never get another chance.

"You were seen coming up from the dungeons, boy," Fallon was saying. "Then we take you down there and find our little prisoners gone. Explain."

"I didn't let them go, Fallon. I was going to, but they were already gone," Peter said, his voice filled with pain.

It took all of Alick's willpower not to fling the door open and run in to stop his suffering. "Hurry, Karter," Alick whispered. There was so much adrenaline in her system, she could barely feel anything anymore. A loud clattering sounded in the hall beyond the far door.

"What was that?" Fallon snapped at the guards. One of them went to the door and opened it just as Karter went dashing past the entrance.

"It's the boy!" The guard yelled.

"Well, don't just stand there, go catch them!" Fallon snarled. "The girl will not survive again!" And like magic, the four guards slipped out of the door to chase Karter. Alick just hoped that he was faster than they were.

Alick opened the door a little bit more, enough that her whole face showed, just as Peter looked up. Luckily, his gasp was masked by the guards shoving him to the ground.

"You see, we always get what we want," Fallon said with as close to a smile as he ever got. "For your lack of cooperation, however, I'm afraid your life will not be spared."

Alick watched as Peter got up off the ground, took a look, and saw the two soldiers still left and Fallon, advancing toward him with his sword.

"Okay, okay, you win, I'll squeal," Peter gasped.

"Too late for that, my dear boy, we're already on their tails."

"No! It's a trick! You're only chasing the boy, Karter."

Fallon stopped where he was and narrowed his eyes. "And why should I believe you?" he hissed.

"Because you know Alick's smart enough not to just go running past the room she knows you're in."

Alick bit her lip, what was Peter doing? Would he really betray her in return for his life?

Fallon pondered what Peter had said. "Well then, where would she be?" he asked, a dangerous undercurrent to his words.

Peter caught Alick's eye as he answered. "She's above us. Waiting for the right moment to blast through the ceiling and attack." Alick let herself breathe again. It was a dangerous play on Peter's part; as soon as they figured out the trick, he was dead. But then Alick realized the beauty of his plan.

"You two go check it out," Fallon ordered the remaining soldiers.

"What about him?" one asked.

"He's not going anywhere," Fallon dismissed. "He doesn't have the strength."

The two soldiers left, and Alick let out a silent cry of thanks. Peter had done exactly what Alick needed: Fallon was alone.

CHAPTER 38

Rubble-and-rock-littered stairs, a large gaping hole, and huge boulder replaced the door Karter scrambled through, coughing from the dust. Behind him, he heard the four guards yelling at each other, but it was the sight in front of him that captured Karter's attention.

The night was alive with color. The black of Fallon's soldiers below on the ground; the red and yellow of the flames as they licked the castle walls and ran up entire columns, casting a glow on everyone; the blue and green garb of the Pantasmas, the brown of the wood, and the grey of steel and rock littering the battleground. Karter lunged forward and knocked a Pantasma girl out of the way of a boulder as it was catapulted onto the balcony.

"Be careful, Skye!" Karter yelled. He pulled the girl up and pulled her along with him, away from the soldiers that had cleared the boulder in the stairwell and were quickly closing the gap.

"Get down!" Skye yelled. She suddenly dove to the ground, taking Karter with her, as dragon fire burst through their end of the hallway and barbecued the four soldiers.

"Thanks," Karter called. Skye saluted and ran off, firing several arrows down toward the ground as she did so. The balcony was complete chaos. Everywhere Karter looked, Pantasmas were diving out of the way of various projectiles, running forward occasionally in groups of five or six to dislodge the ladders that kept popping up bearing Fallon's men. On the ground, troops of the soldier's marched, using their three catapults to try and keep the Pantasmas back long enough to get a ladder up and their men onto the balcony. Meanwhile, the two dragons stomped through their ranks, blasting lines of men at once, and causing chaos wherever they stepped.

The sounds were deafening.

Karter clapped his hands over his ears as a particularly large boulder shattered into the side of the castle below him.

"Team seven to the front, there's a ladder coming!" A familiar voice cut through the din.

Karter shot his head up and saw Rydly standing near the back wall. One side of his face was really cut up and his shirt had several burn holes, but other than that, he looked perfectly fine. At Rydly's command, a small group of Pantasmas scrambled to the front of the balcony. Three of the kids started shooting arrows repeatedly down the side of the castle while two others grabbed the ends of the ladder and shoved as hard as they could, sending it falling straight back down the way it had come.

"Rydly," Karter called, running through the flying debris to his friend.

"Karter! Where's Alick?!"

"With Fallon. I had to create a distraction. Where's Sam?"

"She should be down by the front door with the rest of the Pantasmas."

"Have they been ramming it?"

"Yes, they broke through just recently. I sent down reinforcements." Another ladder came up, this one disgorging several soldiers before the Pantasmas managed to knock it down. One of the soldiers came straight for Karter and Rydly, who drew their swords and dispatched the enemy within a couple minutes. A sudden commotion drew Karter's attention to the doors on the castle side of the balcony.

"What's that?" Rydly asked before the doors burst open and a flood of Pantasmas burst onto the balcony. They were followed by several soldiers before the doors could be shut again.

"Barricade the doors with all we have! We're surrounded!"

"Sam!" Rydly yelled. The girl in question emerged from the haze, a wild look in her eyes, ordering the panicked Pantasmas about while doing her best to dispatch as many of the soldiers as she could.

Karter and Rydly lunged into action, helping barricade the doors and dispatch the enemy. When a small lull was reached, Rydly grabbed Sam.

"What happened?"

"After the door broke down, we couldn't hold. There were too many of them. It would've been a slaughter, Rydly. We had to retreat."

Karter clenched his jaw. "So the soldiers are in the castle, and we're surrounded on a balcony that is easy prey from both sides."

Rydly and Sam both nodded.

Karter cursed. "Let's hope Alick hurries," he muttered. And the three of them crashed into the fray.

CHAPTER 39

So much expectation, so much pressure, Alick thought as she watched Fallon from the passageway. All she had to do was spring out and stick a sword through him, and all of it would be over. Everything Alick had gained, her new family, her new friends, her new life, all of it would be saved. She just had to jump out and do it. Alick drew her sword and leaned against the door, willing it to slide open all the way.

Peter saw what she was doing; Alick could see it in his eyes. Fallon's focus was on the window, at the battle below, but he was about to turn, about to catch Alick.

"Fallon!" Peter spat suddenly. Alick breathed a sigh of relief. She slipped out of the passage and closed the door behind her, sliding behind a sofa and escaping Fallon's notice. The longer she stayed undetected, the easier this would be.

"What do you want, boy?" Fallon sneered.

Up above, Alick heard the soldier's footsteps. They had reached the room. Alick didn't have much longer.

Fallon heard the footsteps too.

"I wonder, boy, why I hear no struggle. No sudden cry of alarm or explosion as Karenza speeds up her plans. Why do the footsteps seem unhurried and methodical instead of frantic?" Fallon mused aloud, drawing his sword and moving over to where Peter had finally managed to stand. "Did you think you could trick me?" Fallon snarled, grabbing Peter by his shirt and pressing the blade of his sword to his neck.

"Maybe she's hiding," Peter said, looking Fallon straight in the eye.

Alick crawled along the floor, under tables and around lamps; she was almost close enough to Fallon. Just a bit further.

"I don't think so." Fallon began to press the blade into Peter who gave a sharp cry.

"Stop it, Fallon."

Fallon paused and drew his sword back, turning just enough to see Alick.

"Well, now. If it isn't little Karenza. You did lie to me, boy." And before Alick could so much as move a muscle, Fallon took his sword and plunged it through Peter's chest.

"No!" Alick yelled, but it was too late.

"See, Karenza? Look what fighting gets you." Fallon threw Peter to the ground.

"There was no need to do that, Fallon," Alick said, her voice steady, but even she could hear the sobs that were threatening to come. She couldn't think about Peter. She had to hold herself together. *Just focus on Fallon, focus on hate.*

"No?" Fallon taunted, running his thumb along his bloody blade. "But you're going to kill me?"

"If it means saving everyone, yes." Alick took a deep breath and readjusted her footing.

Fallon narrowed his eyes and began to walk. "What sort of society is it that requires more violence to end violence? Sounds like a vicious cycle to me." His drawl was cruel and monotonous, callous and biting. It sent shivers down Alick's spine as it filled the space.

"It's *your* society, Fallon," Alick bit back. "It's *your* fault that this kingdom is such a cruel place."

"Temper, temper, little Karenza. I'm simply doing my job."

"*Your* job?" Alick seethed. "It was never to be *your* job, Fallon. You made it your job. You forced it to be your job. The job was my father's, and it was meant to be mine."

"Oh, so now we're selfish and angry, are we?" Fallon sneered, facing her with his sword. "Enough of this." And he lunged. Alick brought up her blade to block his and countered with a swipe at his side.

"I am doing what's best for my people. You forced my hand, Fallon," Alick panted as she and Fallon crossed blades again and again. She ducked and Fallon's death blow missed her, shattering the nearest lamp. Alick leapt over the sofa and swiped at Fallon's head, succeeding in nicking his cheek.

Fallon wiped at the blood in disgust.

"The crown is mine, Karenza. It always will be. This world dwells in blood and death, dealing out pain and punishment with glory. I would have brought about a new age, a new age where that didn't shock people, an age where I ruled absolute. Your father's pathetic ideals of freedom. Bah. There is only freedom in death," Fallon snarled, lunging again. The battle sounds below them increased, and Alick heard the sound of soldiers' footsteps marching below. "Your time is running out, Karenza. My men have breached the castle. Soon you will all join those that dare to believe that equality and peace can ever have a place in a world full of darkness and greed."

Alick felt panic welling up inside her, replacing the fear that had been gnawing there for several hours. She had hoped that Fallon's sword skills would be rusty, that he hadn't used his blade since becoming King. But Fallon was as sharp a swordsman as ever, and Alick was having difficulty getting shots at him. What did she have to lose? If she didn't kill him now, they were all dead anyway.

"I don't need any more time," Alick replied, and then she threw herself into the fight. Every trick, every move, everything she had ever learned, she used, pressing Fallon relentlessly, not bothering to block any shots he happened to get in, not letting him gain the advantage. It was a great way to get herself killed. But Alick was out of options. So she pressed. She ignored it when Fallon cut her arm and when Fallon put a gash in her leg. She just pressed. Strike, turn, duck, swipe. Always aiming for his chest or head. Life-threatening injuries.

When they were by the stained glass window, Alick saw her opening. She caught Fallon's blade and spun, forcing it to clatter to the ground and pinning him to the window, her sword level with his heart.

"You don't have the strength to kill me," Fallon hissed. "You don't have the stomach."

Alick stared into Fallon's cold eyes, eyes that were already dead, had always been dead. She remembered every horrible thing Fallon had ever done. She remembered the flash of the blade as he had beheaded her father. She remembered watching Pantasmas swing from the gallows because she couldn't get there in time. She remembered Fallon piercing Peter only minutes before.

"It's time you left this world alone, Fallon," she whispered. And by luck, she looked up, out of the stained glass window, just in time to let go of Fallon and dive aside.

Crash!

One of the dragons had knocked into a catapult, throwing off its aim. The boulder came sailing through the stained glass window, throwing Fallon back and imbedding itself in the couch.

Alick coughed from the dust and got up, carefully brushing bits of glass from herself. She quickly scanned the room for Fallon and found him on the floor not ten feet away.

She ran over, knowing as soon as she saw him that the wounds were mortal. Large pieces of glass were lodged in his chest, and his head was bleeding excessively from a large gash by the temple.

Alick knelt by his side and Fallon met her eyes. For the first time, Alick saw fear.

"Do you remember the first time we met, Karenza?" Fallon asked, his voice rough and almost human.

Alick shook her head. She didn't.

"I had just arrived to court your aunt, who's dead by the way—"

"What?! When? How?" Alick interrupted, horrified.

"Died a couple years back, fever took her."

"You never told the town," Alick accused.

"Why bother?" Fallon was silent for a while and Alick was beginning to wonder if he'd died when he spoke again. "I arrived in the courtyard just as you were finishing a lesson learning to shoot a bow and arrow. I scoffed at the sight. I told your father not to bother teaching a girl to fight. They weren't ever any good at it."

"Why are you telling me this?" Alick asked.

"Your father told me that day never to underestimate you, Karenza. He was right." Fallon closed his eyes, his voice becoming weaker. "He was right." And just like that, it was over, a decade of terror ended by a stray shot. Historians would probably find something significant in that, proclaim divine providence or something. Alick saw it as karma. Fallon had done such wrong against the world it had finally decided enough was enough.

Alick bit her lip and got up, running over to where Fallon had thrown Peter. His glassy eyes looked up at her. It was too late for him. He was already gone.

"I'm sorry, Peter," Alick whispered, closing his eyes. She took a deep breath and stood up, shutting away her pain deep in the recesses of her brain. It got easier all the time. There would be a time for mourning, when she would sob for everything they'd lost. But right now, she had a war to finish. It was time to seize what they had gained.

CHAPTER 40

Everything was nearly lost. The Pantasmas were completely surrounded. Those that could still stand formed a ring around those who were dead or too injured to fight anymore. Nearly half were incapacitated, and that number was growing rapidly. "Alick, if there was ever a time when you were more needed, I cannot think of it," Karter said aloud as he managed to parry away another death blow.

That was when the dragons cried.

If you have ever been unfortunate enough to hear ten thousand violins being played by six year-olds sawing away at their highest note, then you might have some idea of what the cry sounded like.

Everyone in the castle stopped what they were doing to cover their ears and the battle stopped instantly. When the dragons ceased, only one voice could be heard: Alick, standing on the turret above the castle gate, her voice amplified by the same mechanism Fallon used on Heritor Day to address the town. Above her, the blue dragon flew around the castle, carrying the lifeless body of William Derex Fallon is its claws.

"Fallon is dead. The war is won," Alick was saying. "Drop your arms and retreat. According to the proclamations lain down by the Witch of Sombras in the laws of Heritor Day, you have surrendered. I am your new Queen."

Karter smiled, a large grin that took up his entire face. He turned to Rydly and Sam.

"She did it."

"She did it," they replied synchronously with equal wonder. The cheer that went up from the Pantasmas, the castle workers, and the village was deafening, and they all began shouting the same thing. *Alick.* Over and over again they chanted, as the soldiers bowed down, recognizing their new ruler. It was surreal, the idea that the reign of terror could be over was incomprehensible. But it was over, and no one could deny that hard as it was.

Karter called to his dragon and clambered on while the rest of the Pantasmas, who could still walk, ran down through the castle and out onto the lawn, toward the tower where Alick stood alone. Karter was the first to reach it, with Sam and Rydly hot on his heels.

The three of them practically tackled Alick, hugging her and congratulating her.

"You did it, Alick," Karter said, the knowledge still not quite sinking in.

Alick smiled. It was an exhausted, worn smile, but it was still a smile. "Thanks to you guys," she said. By this time, the rest of the Pantasmas had reached the top of the tower and together the band of thieves looked out over their kingdom. To Fallon's soldiers, whose allegiances defaulted to Alick, and to the townspeople, whose dreams had come true that night.

Fallon was gone. And in that moment, it wasn't just Alick who had won. It was everyone. And in that moment, it wasn't Alick who reigned, it was band of thieves in royal colors who refused to give up.

Karter positioned himself next to Alick and grabbed her hand. Alick turned to him, smiling again, and this time Karter could see it was a happy smile. A cry went up, and the two of them looked over the balcony and saw that the younger

Pantasmas were coming, led by Tara and Kara, walking through the crowd to join their leader in triumph.

When they had reached the top of the tower, Alick held her hands up over the crowd to quiet them, waiting until they had shushed to make the flame symbol: the symbol of dragons, of her family, and of Libre.

Karter raised his hands above his head and did the same. Like a ripple, it spread out through the gathered people until every man, woman, and child gathered had raised the flame to the sky. It was over. It was really and truly over. And as they stood there, the sunrise came, bathing everyone in its soft, golden light. Karter smiled. Libre was born anew.

A small nudge brought Karter's focus down to Piper, who had snuck through the crowd to be next to Alick. Alick took one look at the small girl and leaned down to lift her up. Together they remade the flame symbol, Piper's small hand struggling to meet Alick's. And in the silence, Karter heard Piper's small voice as she whispered to Alick, "I told you they could never forget you. You're our hero."

The day was a blur; so much destruction had been wreaked in the night that it was hard to believe things could ever truly be resolved. But slowly the bodies were found, the injured tended to, and the dead buried. Karter rarely saw Alick as she was hurried about the place settling everything. She would be a good ruler.

As the day wore on, Karter found himself in the throne room, looking at a picture of Alick and her parents while soldiers bustled around removing all traces of Fallon from the room.

"I was so young then." Alick's voice penetrated Karter's thoughts and he whipped around.

"It's good to see you, Alick," he said, and he meant it.

Alick gave a weary chuckle. "Let's take a walk, Karter. I need a break. I've had to watch too many friends laid to rest today."

Karter agreed, and soon they were walking around the castle grounds, picking their way through scorched grass and bit of the castle wall.

Alick forged ahead, and Karter found her sitting on a particularly large piece of rubble, looking at the necklace she had shown him in the dungeon.

"You never did tell me why that had my family crest on it," Karter said as he sat down beside her. He brushed a stray hair of hers aside and remembered the moment in the passageway when he'd almost kissed her.

"It was a betrothal gift," Alick finally said.

Karter let that sink in. "You were betrothed," he said, drawing back.

Alick nodded.

"To my brother," Karter said. His heart felt like it was breaking in two. He'd come so far and done so much, and his brother was still ruining his life.

"No, actually."

"What?" Karter snapped his head up.

"I wasn't betrothed to the heir of Outeiro. I was betrothed to his brother," Alick whispered, looking so vulnerable in that instant that it took all of Karter's strength not to put his arm around her.

Flashes of memory began flickering in Karter's mind as what Alick said sank in.

"When I was young," he began, struggling to remember, "I asked my mother why I wasn't betrothed. Why Balthazar was and I wasn't."

"What did she say?"

"She said I had been, but the girl had died." Karter looked over at Alick. "But you didn't die," he whispered.

Alick shook her head. "No, I didn't," she said with a little laugh.

"I guess that makes you my fiancé," Karter continued, his heart beating faster and faster. He was entering dangerous territory.

Alick shrugged. "You don't have to marry me if you don't want," she said, studying her shoes. "The arrangement was made by our parents. Mine are dead and yours banished you. They're not exactly around to insist."

Karter shook his head no repeatedly and pulled Alick to her feet. He looked into her eyes and leaned close.

"Alick Karenza Daveney, I can think of no one else I ever want to spend my days with. It may have been our parents' arrangement, but that's just luck and happenstance. I've never met anyone else like you, Alick. And I never will."

Alick looked up at him in wonder, and Karter smiled. Her eyes had never been so beautiful. He leaned in until his lips met hers, kissing her gently.

"Marry me," he whispered.

"Aren't we supposed to court first?" He felt her smile and he leaned away far enough to see her eyes challenging him.

"You don't think battling dragons together counts?" He was teasing her.

Karter held his breath as he watched Alick's face. He had hoped that in trying to get out of their engagement, Alick had simply been expressing doubts that he loved her. He couldn't stand to think she might not feel the same way about him.

"Yes," Alick finally whispered. Then she smiled. "Yes, Karter I will marry you, eventually."

Karter smiled and stood up. "You know what, Alick?" he asked, running one hand through her hair.

"What?" Alick replied playfully, wrapping her arms around him.

"I'm kind of glad my parent's banished me," Karter whispered.

Alick laughed and stood on her tiptoes, reaching up to meet him, and while their dragons wheeled overhead, they kissed.

EPILOGUE

"Hurry up, Alick!" Sam called through the door. "You're going to be late."

Alick smiled at herself in the mirror and then met Sam at the door.

"You look fancy," her friend commented as Alick emerged. Alick laughed. It was true that she was wearing fancier clothing than she'd worn in a decade. It was the first time she'd dressed the part of Queen. Subconsciously, she smoothed the long, dark blue velvet dress she was wearing that made her eyes stand out and looked nice with her blonde hair.

"I see you decided to dress for work," Alick replied as the two of them walked down the hall toward the grand ballroom.

Sam flicked her ponytail over her shoulder and glanced down at her outfit. Upon assuming

341

command of the armies, the first thing Alick had done was make Sam the general, and Alick's second in command was currently bedecked in full ceremonial military garb.

"Yeah, well, I was never a dress girl," Sam said with a shrug.

Alick rolled her eyes and took a deep breath. They were here.

"You ready for this?" Sam asked.

Alick nodded. It had been three months since the Battle for Libre, as it had come to be called. The castle had been rebuilt; the two dozen Pantasmas who had died lain to rest. Those Pantasmas with families in the village had been reunited on a day that still filled Alick with happiness as she remembered all the joyous faces of long lost families together again. Those Pantasmas who had no family, like Sam, Rydly, Tara, Kara, and Robin, had found jobs in the castle. Piper was the exception. Too young for work and as alone as Alick had been at that age, Alick had taken her in. She lived in the palace with the head housekeeper and was almost always on Alick's heels.

The economy was on its way back up. Alick had made contact with Outeiro, reopening the trade that had once existed between them. It would be a long time before the kingdom was back to its former glory, but they were on their way. The dragons had stayed too which had been a huge help; especially with rebuilding the castle.

The door in front of Alick opened up, and Alick began the long procession down the aisle.

At the end, waiting for her, were the priest, Karter, Rydly, and her throne. Alick smiled. Karter was a commander under Sam, a special commission for three years before their wedding would render him King. Alick had offered Rydly command in the army as well, but he opted to take over for Locque, the castle butler.

Rydly would oversee all operations under the castle roof. Alick had been unsure at first, but Rydly loved the job and being close to his girlfriend. He never had liked conflict, but he was a great leader. Managing the castle was perfect for him.

Alick snuck a glance at Sam walking resolutely beside her. She still couldn't believe her two best friends were dating, but Karter had been right. As soon as they began courting, Sam had become instantly nicer to Rydly, the only sign that they had ever grated on each other's nerves was that Sam still called Rydly Riddle, though much more endearingly.

Alick reached the end of the aisle and turned, facing her people. Since the end of the battle, they had all come to know of her heritage and her parents. Any lingering feelings among the people that she might not deserve the crown had evaporated upon them discovering she was the lost princess.

"Do you, the people, accept Alick Karenza Daveney as your rightful ruler, to look out for your well-being and govern the affairs of Libre?" The priest began, addressing the gathered crowd.

"We do."

"Do you, Alick Karenza Daveney, agree to govern the people of Libre fairly and according to the laws of the kingdom?"

"Yes," Alick replied.

"Will you uphold justice and use mercy in execution of your judgement?"

"I will."

"Then I hereby crown you, Alick Karenza Daveney, Queen and Protecter of Libre."

The priest came forward and placed Alick's father's crown upon her head. She had been surprised to find it in a closet a few days ago, but she was glad she had. Alick had never felt closer to her parents.

"All hail the Queen," the priest finished, and row by row, people bowed.

Alick walked back down the aisle slowly, as confetti fell from the ceiling and the anthem of Libre played, her people singing along.

Today would wind up being a holiday, she was sure. The coronation of a new age.

Alick reached the end of the hall and made her way up the stairs until she was on the balcony overlooking the ballroom.

There was one last duty she had before the ceremony was over, before she was officially their Queen. Alick raised her scepter into the air and yelled, "Long live Libre!" and as Alick left, she could here the peoples response echoing behind her.

"Long live freedom!"